BABY CAKES

THE COMPLETE BITE SERIES

S.J. TILLY

The Complete Bite Series

Baby Cakes

A collection of Tilly World Novellas

Cover: Lori Jackson Design

Cover photographer and model: Wander Aguiar

Editors: Jeanine Harrell, Indie Edits with Jeanine

& Beth Lawton, VB Edits

*Baby Cakes, specifically the cover, is dedicated to
all of my hungry ho ho ho's.
I promise to always keep you fed.*

SECOND BITE

A Tilly World Holiday Novella

S.J. TILLY

SECOND BITE - PART 1

By S.J. Tilly

Second Bite

A Tilly World Novella

Cover: James Adkinson
Editor: Jeanine Harrell—Indie Edits with Jeanine

This book is dedicated to the winter of 2021, when I spent way too much time binge watching GBBO and obsessing over the P. Hollywood gaze.

ALICE

"*P*laces, everyone!"

Oh god, oh god, oh god.

"We're going live in three... two..." The man behind the camera holds up a single finger.

The big light in the front of the room flashes red.

And my heart stops.

Oh, sweet Santa, my heart has stopped.

I shove my fists into the pockets of my dress, not wanting my trembling hands to be the first thing that millions of viewers see.

"Hello and welcome to *Second Bite!*" a voice I recognize as Joey's, the show's good-looking host, calls out. "Thank you for joining us for what I'm sure will be an amazing holiday special."

Handsome in a boy-next-door kind of way, Joey is the reason that lots of people watch *Second Bite*. But he's never been my reason. Just like he's not the reason that my pulse is galloping through my veins.

"Before we introduce you to the contestants, let's bring the judges out here."

Holy crap, it's happening!

The judges are the reason for my current state. Or rather, one judge, in particular, is the reason for... everything.

The reason I get up in the morning.

The reason I'm here.

The reason I freaking breathe.

My fingers squeeze around the lucky silver dollar in my pocket in a vain attempt to center myself.

Calm down, Alice.

Joey's standing with his back to me and the other contestants at the front of the large room, so we're the backdrop for this live introduction.

The room is half stage, half warehouse, with bright lights glaring down on the four individual baking stations. And on TV, it looks cozy. Intimate. But being here on set, it feels like a whole different world. A terrifying, over-lit, nothing-to-hide-behind world.

I hear Joey introduce Pamela, the sweet female judge in her seventies who rarely has a negative word to say to anyone and almost always has a glass of wine in her hand. And I try to focus. I really do. But now, seconds before seeing the man I've been in love with for years, I'm rethinking every single decision I've made in my life. Starting with this dress.

With my hands still in my pockets, I try to pull it down, just a little bit more.

My cousins said this dress was cute. That the pink and red striped wrap dress was festive without being too *on the nose*. But I'm starting to think that my cousins are idiots. After all, they're the ones who signed me up for this nightmare.

Meet your hero! Bat your lashes at Chef Kesso! Throw your panties at Chef Kesso!

They kept trying to tell me how great it'd be to meet him, as if I needed any convincing of that. No, it's the actual performing and competing part that adds a whole new level of stress to an already nerve-racking introduction.

But he doesn't know that you're obsessed with him, I remind myself for the hundredth time. He won't know that you're slipping into cardiac arrest just because he's close.

Joey claps once. "And here's the Scrooge himself, Mike Kesso."

My eyes snap up to the front, and this time my heart really does stop. Because standing there, just a few feet away, is world famous Pastry Chef Mike Kesso.

Be still, my soul.

He's here.

But I don't think of him as Mike. Ever since that "Meet the Judges" episode aired a few seasons back, I've only been able to think of him as Michael. All because he made an offhand comment about how only his work acquaintances call him Mike and that his close friends and family call him Michael. So, in my fantasies, that's what I call him.

Michael.

Only this isn't a fantasy. This is real. He's real, and he's so close I want to wrap my arms around him and feel his body heat just to make sure.

Joey is saying something, but I can't tear my eyes—or attention—away from Michael.

He looks exactly like he does on TV—dark eyes, dark hair that's graying at the temples, and wearing his signature black shirt with the sleeves rolled up to his elbows. And with his arms crossed over his chest, I can see just enough of his sleeve tattoos to have my thighs pressing together.

My mouth starts to salivate, and I tug down on the material one more time, wanting to hide my legs as they try to squeeze the growing ache away.

Wearing a dress was a bad idea.

A very, very bad idea.

3

MICHAEL

"*A*re you fucking kidding me?" I growl into the phone, not caring that we're going to start airing any moment.

"Look, Mike, I know it's not what you wanted—" My manager tries to placate me.

"Not what I wanted? This is so far from what I wanted it's not even funny."

"I know, but New Year's in Canada isn't so—"

I cut him off. "If you don't want me to fire you, you won't finish that sentence." He wisely stays silent. "I told you I wanted a break. I told you I didn't want to do any of these fucking holiday specials. And now you have me shooting some live stream bullshit over the next three days—which is gonna be a goddamn nightmare—and then instead of going home to re-fucking-lax after this circus, you're telling me I need to go to Canada and do it all over again."

"I know, I'm sorry. But after this, I promise you'll have two months off." He pauses. "One, at least."

I almost laugh.

"If you're lonely, we can arrange to have some of your family meet you in Winnipeg, or I can always have a, um, a *lady* waiting for you."

I pinch the bridge of my nose. "Did you seriously just offer to send me a Canadian prostitute?"

"She doesn't have to be Cana—"

I hang up the phone.

How? How have I surrounded myself with such idiots?

But I know it's not just the schedule that's getting to me. It's... *fuck.*

I heave out a breath.

It's the loneliness.

I don't want a random hookup. I don't need a *professional* to meet me in Canada. I need a life. A real life with real people and a real relationship.

We all grow up romanticizing fame, thinking it's the pinnacle of success. And sure, it can be. It's validating, and my money and fame have opened a lot of doors. But they've closed just as many.

"We're going live in..."

I sigh.

Time to get my head out of my ass because I have a job to do. And angry or not, I won't just walk away.

My palms smooth out the front of my shirt.

Might as well throw myself into work. I have nothing else to do. Even though I won't meet the love of my life on *Second fucking Bite.*

ALICE

hey're at the second table. The judges and the host are at the second table doing the contestant intros, and I'm dying. I'm absolutely dying.

Michael has looked a little upset since he walked onto the set, and it's only adding to my stress.

I mean, he always looks kinda pissed. That's his demeanor. But this is different. Like maybe something bad happened in his personal life. And I don't like that. I want to help him, make him feel better. Maybe give him a hug.

The idea almost makes me laugh. Pretty sure if I tried to hug *The* Mike Kesso, he'd whip out a spatula from some hidden pocket and slap it against my forehead, holding me out of reach.

I shift on my feet as they move to the back row of baking stations—*my row*—heading to my neighbor's table first.

Her name is Mikayla, and she's beautiful. Thin where I'm... not. Smooth chocolate-colored hair to my messy blonde curls. Wearing a skintight ribbon red dress that you might see in a lawyer show rather than my girly, flowy one. She even has heels on. *Heels!* Already inches taller than me, they make her almost the same height as Michael. Where I barely come up to his shoulder in my little white tennis shoes.

If I thought I was worried about what Michael might think of my appearance before, that worry has turned into a full-blown phobia.

Not like I thought he'd take one look at me and hearts would fill his eyes. But next to her... well, next to her, I feel hopeless.

Seriously, it's like they lined us up this way on purpose.

Right in front of me in the first row is an older, kind-faced gentleman, Hugh. And next to him is a polished, pushing-thirty man named Brent. I heard something about him being an executive assistant for some big wig, and it must be true, because he looks the part.

Basically, we've been put into a grid. Look at us one way, and it's men, then women. Or turn us on our axis and you have frumpy, then sleek.

Nerves shot to hell, I have to force my hands out of my pockets when I see the trio start to turn my way.

I try to devote glances to Joey and Pamela, but my attention is all on Michael.

Except he's not even looking up. His eyes are lowered, one hand reaching across his broad torso to adjust the chunky watch on his opposite wrist.

"Our last and final contestant, Alice Hatter." Joey introduces me, making sure not to step in front of the cameraman following him around.

Smiling my response—since words are hard—I shake his hand, then Pamela's.

Not sure if I'm supposed to or not, I hold my hand out in Michael's direction.

But he's still not paying attention.

My hand wavers in the air.

"So..." Joey's voice is overly bright, clearly feeling the discomfort of Chef Kesso's inattention. "I hear you work in IT."

My cheeks heat. *IT? Did my cousins seriously fill out my application saying I worked in IT?*

My head gives a slow nod, because what else am I supposed to say? *No, sorry. I wasn't actually the one who applied to be here, and working a soul-sucking job as a telemarketer is hardly IT. Even if it was, the company went under last week, and I've finally accepted that my last three paychecks that bounced are never going to be replaced. And since I can't afford rent without my shitty job, I'm moving out at the end of the week and into my traitor cousins' basement. But yeah, I work in IT.*

Joey clears his throat. "And that someday, you'd like to own a bakery." Joey fills the awkward silence.

I almost snort. Bakery? *I don't even own a reliable car.*

"Yeah, I'd like that." My voice comes out quiet, and I realize I'm still holding my hand out like a fool.

I start to lower my hand and then miss whatever Joey says next because Michael raises his eyes. And when they meet mine, I freeze.

MICHAEL

"*J*'d like that." The feminine voice spears into my chest, and my eyes snap up.

Holy holiday heaven.

Standing before me is a lush-as-fuck angel with evergreen eyes, berry-red lips, and a body I'd write to Santa for.

Her hand is retracting as though she'd given up reaching for me. Before I can consider the consequences, I dart my own hand out, clasping her palm in mine. And the second we touch, a volt of awareness rockets down my spine.

Startled by my sudden movement, she lets out a small gasp, and I swear I feel her inhale deep in my balls.

"What's your name?" I growl, tightening my grip.

Joey clears his throat next to me. I'm sure he already said her name, but I wasn't listening. That last contestant was trying to openly flirt, and it annoyed the shit out of me. So I came over here with my head down and my inner voice grumbling, and I regret every second I've wasted not looking at this wonderful woman. But I don't want to hear Joey tell me her name. I want to hear it from her mesmerizing lips.

I flex my fingers and her mouth pops open.

"I'm Alice."

Her whispered voice is all the confirmation I need. This woman is mine, and I'm gonna find a way to keep her.

ALICE

He's touching me.
Michael Kesso is touching me. Holding my hand.
And it feels as sensual as if his hand was down my panties.

"I'm Mike." He introduces himself, as though I don't have his photo next to my bed and his entire bio memorized.

"Hi." I breathe the word.

"Hi." His simple reply goes straight to my core.

Hi.

I'm going to hear his voice in my sleep.

I don't know what I thought would happen when we met, but... touching him? Direct eye contact? I didn't prepare for this.

So, I do the only thing I can do when my crush is standing in front of me, holding my hand. I smile.

Then I stumble forward.

I bump into my workstation, slapping my free hand down on the countertop to catch my balance.

Michael lets go of my hand, and the people around us startle at my flailing.

And that's how I die.

Embarrassment manifests as a Lake Placid–sized crocodile, and it swallows me down whole. I disappear. The crocodile eats the cameras. And no one ever witnesses The Stumble That Ended Alice's Life.

With burning cheeks, I drop my eyes, and I do my best to ignore the other contestants' snickering.

"Alrighty then." Joey claps his hands together. "Let's get this show on the road!"

Keeping my head tipped down, I nod.

That's a great idea! Let's add high-stakes competition to the garbage fire of emotions already blazing in my stomach.

I watch the trio walk to the front of the room, and as Joey explains the first challenge, I glance down at my empty hands. Because I could've sworn that Michael pulled me toward him.

MICHAEL

He's too fucking close.
        My jaw flexes.
If he doesn't back the fuck off, I'm going to—

A cracking sound reaches my ears, and I loosen my grip on the wooden spoon I'd absently picked up.

If you break it in half, the jagged edges could work well as a shiv.

I drop the spoon onto the judges' table and stride down the aisle between the contestants' stations. Toward the camera crew. Toward Alice.

These competitions started out fun. Then they got a little monotonous. And now, today, I'm experiencing a level of stress I never knew existed. It feels like anxiety, excitement, dread, doubt, and impatience all rolled into one.

It's been so long since I've been anything other than completely sure of myself, and I don't quite remember how to deal with it.

I want this woman. Correction, *need* this woman. And if the flush in her cheeks and sparkle in her eye is any indication, she wants me too. I just need to make her need me. Make her burn from the inside out, incinerating whatever walls she might have, and allow me access to every part of her being.

My heavy footfalls don't go unnoticed, and I feel the other bakers watching me walk past.

Don't fuck this up for her.

Reluctantly, I slow.

I need to listen to the small voice of my conscience, for once, and wait. I don't know what Alice's skill level is, but no one makes it on this show if they don't deserve it. And if I make it obvious that I desire her, if I get her underneath me before the competition is done and ruin her chances of winning, or taint her win with rumors, I'd never forgive myself.

By the time I stop in front of her counter, I've made up my mind. I'll treat her like any other contestant. I have to. Because with these cameras live streaming everything, there's no editing. I can't mess up. So, usual prick personality it is.

"Chef Mike." Joey angles his body, giving me room to fit between him and Pamela. "Perfect timing. Alice here was just about to tell us what she's making."

Her wide green eyes meet mine, and, for a long second, I wonder if throwing her over my shoulder and walking out of here would really be that big of a deal.

She blinks at me, her hands stilling over the bowl of unmixed ingredients. "Are you ready?"

I clamp my teeth together, trapping a groan in my throat. *Yeah, Baby Cakes, I'm fucking ready.*

Joey chokes, then pats himself on the chest. "We're ready, darling."

I throw a glare at him before focusing back on the angel in front of me. If Joey thinks he can give her pet names and win her affections with his fake-ass charm, he's gonna be thinking differently when I shove a whisk down his smarmy throat.

"Okay." Alice licks her lips, and I feel myself leaning forward.

"I'm making a red velvet, white chocolate swirl cake, topped with peppermint-vanilla cream cheese frosting."

Joey rubs his stomach. "That sounds like a sugar rush!"

She smiles at Joey, and it makes me want to punch him in the face.

"It's sweet." Alice lifts one intriguing shoulder. "But I'm of the belief that desserts should be sweet. And I think the combination of flavors gives the palate enough to focus on without leaving time to worry about sugar."

All heads turn to face me, waiting for my input. And I clasp my left wrist with my right hand and hold them in front of my groin. I'm sure I look disinterested, but I need to cover my growing cock before anyone notices.

"Sounds interesting." I nod to Alice, then turn away. Forcing my focus onto anything else and away from the blood rushing to my dick.

Too sweet indeed.

ALICE

*M*y heart plummets to my feet, and my movements freeze. Or mostly freeze, because I'm staring down at clouds of flour as they plume over the edge of the measuring cup in my shaking hands.

Interesting.

I know what that means. *Interesting* means he thinks it sounds bad.

I look at the half-started batter and feel my shoulders slump.

A utensil elsewhere clatters against the floor, and I glance up, finding one of the camera guys still standing in front of my counter. Camera aimed right at my face.

The color drains from my cheeks, and I drop my head back down, feeling defeated before I've even really started.

And what was with that introduction? Am I just reading into it because I have the biggest crush in the world on him? Or was he acting... different?

I exhale. The test batches turned out well.

Trust yourself.

I roll my eyes. Yeah, *trust myself.* Because that's gone so well in the past.

But there's no changing my plan now. Michael might not like what I make, but it's too late to come up with something else.

Shaking off the bad feelings rolling around in my shoulders, I dump the rest of the flour into the bowl and get to work.

"THIRTY MINUTES LEFT!"

Okay, focus, Alice.

"Ten minutes left!"

Almost there. You can do this.

"One minute left!"

Oh, holy shit! Hurry!

STARING down at my platter of mini cakes, I worry my lip.

They don't look as pristine as I'd like, but they're still pretty clean. The frosting is holding its shape, and the pulled sugar bows—that I made right up until the last second—don't look terrible. All in all, they look like the tiny presents I'd intended, and I feel semi-confident that the judges will like them.

I probably should've listened to the judge's reactions toward the first two bakers since they're already on the third, but the adrenaline pumping through my body made that impossible.

A high-pitched giggle yanks my attention to the contestant next to me.

Mikayla has her head thrown back, her long, lean neck stretched out for the cameras. For the host. For Michael.

I slide my hand into my pocket, letting my fingers brush over my lucky coin, while I remind myself that this isn't a beauty contest. I've watched enough episodes to know that the best baker always wins. And I've watched enough of the past bakers on the show attempt to flirt with Michael to know that he never reciprocates.

But maybe that's just because those episodes have all been edited? Maybe in real life, he... acts differently.

I clutch the coin in my fist.

You're here to compete for a baking title. Not a husband.

Lost in my own unraveling thoughts, I once again miss their feedback and find it's suddenly my turn.

As the three staples of *Second Bite* walk my way, I take a few deep, slow breaths.

You got this.

It's just like bringing dessert to a family dinner.

And having that family be brutally honest about it on live TV.

"Remind us what you made here." Joey nods his head toward my display.

I do my best to not think about the cameras looming close, and I keep my voice as level as possible as I walk through the recipe one more time. I gesture, smile, make eye contact with everyone but Michael... totally normal stuff.

I feel like I'm actually doing great. Then I point to one of the cakes, bumping it with my finger and putting a small dent in the frosting.

"Ope!" I jerk my hand back like I touched flames instead of whipped sugar.

Without thinking, I shove my fingertip into my mouth, sucking off the frosting. And, of course, *that's* when I finally look at Michael and lock eyes with his crackling gaze.

My lips pop open, creating an O, and I withdraw my finger.

"Sorry!" I squeak and repeat the apology. "So sorry!"

Michael—*Mike, you need to call him Mike*—works his jaw before plating two of the mini cakes for himself and Pamela.

Great, this is it—zero hour—and you've already offended your celebrity crush with your lack of hygiene.

"Promise I didn't lick those!" I joke, but Pamela is the only one who humors me with a laugh.

Shoving my hands back in my dress pockets, I clamp my lips together and hold my breath.

They pick up their forks, both adjusting the small plates until they're centered in front of them.

My eyes dart between the two judges.

Why is this taking so long?

Does it always take this long?

Pamela lifts her bite first and lets out a sound of surprised appreciation while giving me a nod.

Exhaling, my nerves settle the smallest amount. Until, just like before, my eyes are drawn to Michael's.

He keeps his gaze on mine as he parts his lips and slides the forkful of cake into his mouth.

The move is so carnal a tremor rolls through my body.

He's about to do it.

Michael Kesso is about to taste me.

My eyes widen.

Cake! He's about to taste my cake!

MICHAEL

ucking hell, if this woman doesn't tamp down her reactions, I'm gonna do something to embarrass us both.

A riot of flavors bursts across my tongue, and I'm forced to look away from Alice's wide eyes as my own drop to the plate.

I reach out and fill another forkful, getting more of the cake this time.

I wasn't expecting to like this. I was certain it'd have too many overbearing flavors. But all the elements combine perfectly, embodying the holiday treat we asked for.

My co-judge is talking about balance and notes of vanilla, but I'm still too busy licking my fork off to comment.

I'm pulling the utensil from my lips when a small sound leaves Alice's mouth from across the counter, causing my body to go rigid.

Jesus Christ, did she just fucking whimper?

Because she was watching me?

I clear my throat as I set my fork down. "It's very nice."

It's better than nice, and I see the glances people are giving me and the fork I just set down. But it's not quite *that* good. Not *Second Bite* good. But it's damn close.

20

I hosted a special on the Baking Network years ago before this show was created, and after trying an amazing cake, I picked my fork back up to take a "second bite." It's a misnomer since I take multiple bites when I'm trying something to get the full experience. But if a creation is so good that I pick my fork back up to take another bite, it gets the Second Bite label. People liked it, so the name stuck. So when the idea for this show was laid out, it seemed like the obvious title.

"Okay," Alice murmurs in reply.

Her exhaled word stabs me in the chest. *It's very nice,* isn't feedback. It's crap.

I clear my throat. "The amount of peppermint is just right. Subtle enough that it doesn't overpower, but still distinct." The memory of her licking the frosting off her finger springs to mind, and I try to think of something else to add. "Could be cleaner."

The bright look of pride that had been growing on her features halts.

Fucking hell.

Alice presses her plump lips together and nods her head, not looking sad, just contemplative. Like she's memorizing every word I've said and filing it away for later.

I shift my weight.

I can't leave her with a negative comment. I just can't.

My chin dips, and I tip my head toward the remaining cakes. "Good job."

Before I can make this any more fucking awkward, I turn and walk away from Alice's station.

Good job? That's the best I could come up with?

ALICE

He thinks I did good.
    Michael ate my cake—put it in his mouth and swallowed—and said it was good.

My heart is hammering inside my ribs. I'm tempted to try and hold it in by pressing my hands to my chest, but Joey's standing just in front of my little counter, addressing the cameras for the end of the episode, and I don't want to be caught acting like a total fool on TV.

It's stressful to have the cameras here, especially since I know it's all airing live, and there's no chance for an edit or a redo. But as the afternoon went on, I found myself getting kinda used to them. Probably because all the people carrying the cameras are really nice and good at making me feel welcome. But right now, with Michael's words rattling around in my head, I don't know what to do with myself. It's like one little compliment has made me completely forget how to act normal.

Needing something to do, I start to organize my workspace.

In the normal in-season episodes, there's clearly a break between when the timer goes off and the tasting because the workstations are always pristine. But people cleaning isn't really something the network wants to live stream, so all the stations are in a bit of disarray.

And I'm glad because it gives me something to do with my hands. *Stack dirty pans? Sure!* Anything to keep myself from happy crying over an arguably underwhelming compliment. Or worse yet, tearing my dress off and climbing the unsuspecting Michael like a cat on a Christmas tree—all claws and no finesse.

MICHAEL

*T*he whiskey settles on my tongue, and I let the warmth fill my senses before I swallow.

Alice, my Christmas Aphrodite, is sitting so close I can almost smell her sweet sugar scent. But no matter how near she is, she's still out of reach.

I tip my glass back, draining the rest of my drink.

The whole crew is staying in the same hotel, so we're all having a late dinner in the same hotel bar.

It's a nice place, and it's attached to the St. Paul Convention Center that we're using to shoot this special, so it makes everything easy. I might be considered a big shot by some, but I'm not one of those famous, stuck-up types that require fancy-ass accommodations or a certain brand of bottled water. And now more than ever, I'm happy for that fact, because it means I'll be sleeping under the same roof as my Alice.

I shift in my seat, trying to give my dick some breathing room.

A chorus of laughter from the other side of the bar makes my jaw tick.

Most of the crew is over there with the contestants, including Hot Shot Joey.

There aren't many rules for us on the show—since it's usually low drama—but, while we're shooting, the judges are supposed to stay away from the contestants during any downtime. So no eating dinner together. No drinking together. And, sadly, no getting naked together.

I hear more laughter, but when I narrow my gaze, I notice Alice isn't one of the people laughing. She's sitting back in her seat, cradling the same glass of white wine she started with, softly smiling as she glances around the table.

She's the prettiest creature I've ever seen, and I can't fathom why anyone would let her out in public alone.

If she was mine... That thought trails off.

Does she already belong to someone?

She wasn't wearing a wedding ring. I'm sure of it.

I didn't specifically look, but I'm sure I would've noticed.

My head gives a slow shake.

No, there's no one else.

If there was another man, he's done now. He let her out, let her cross my path, and that's his own fault. Because if she was mine, I'd keep her tied to my side. Literally, if necessary.

I swirl the ice in my glass, wishing I had more alcohol to dull the pounding urge to claim her.

How I'm managing to keep myself from dropping to one knee, and demanding for her hand in marriage, is beyond me.

Pamela nudges my arm while she's saying something to the producer sitting across the table from us, and I nod like I'm listening. But I'm not listening because now Alice is biting her bottom lip. She's biting her lip, and she looks so goddamn fuckable I need to have her.

I'm sliding my chair back from the table before I even register what I'm doing.

What're you gonna do? Just walk over there and ask if she'd like to sit in your lap? Ask to hear what's on her wish list?

Alice's teeth let go, and her lip plumps back into shape, making me groan.

Bed. I need to go to bed.

"You okay?" Pamela asks, mistaking my sound for one of pain.

"Ye—" My answer cuts off when Alice's eyes suddenly lift to meet mine.

She jerks her eyes away, but not before I see the shock covering her features. And the guilt tinting her cheeks.

She was looking for me.

I set my glass down a little harder than necessary and get up.

"See you tomorrow," I grumble to Pamela, pretending it's a proper goodbye, and stride out of the bar.

I need to be alone. In my room.

ALICE

"*H*e's even better in person, eh?"

I startle at the question, nearly spilling my wine.

"Sorry." Brent chuckles, bumping his shoulder into mine. "Didn't mean to scare you. But you know I'm right."

Unbidden, my eyes flicker toward the now empty seat at the judge's table.

He's not wrong. Michael is even hotter in person, but the fact that Brent caught me looking is mortifying. Though it's still not as bad as a second ago when Michael himself caught me.

I sigh and slump in my seat. "You're right."

Brent laughs, clinking his wineglass against mine. "No harm in looking, darling."

With Brent's words rattling around in my brain, I sip the rest of my wine and excuse myself the moment the first person gets up to leave.

I know it's an all-expenses-paid weekend, but I rarely drink, and there's no way I can get through tomorrow if I'm hungover. And even though most of the people are friendly, I don't feel super comfortable with strangers, so the solitude of my room sounds perfect.

Walking out into the lobby, I wave at Pamela when she waves at me, then I hurry my way onto the elevator.

The doors are sliding shut behind me when my purse starts to vibrate with a call.

Smiling, I pull my phone out, not surprised to see it's a Face-Time call.

The elevator's empty, so I answer. "Hey, Suzy."

"Alice!" My cousin, Suzy, and her sister, Sam, cram their faces together to fit on screen. "You were on TV!"

I shake my head, their energy making me feel a little lighter about the stressful day. "Crazy, right?"

"Crazy awesome!" Sam shouts, causing Suzy to wince.

"Chill, woman." Suzy rubs her ear as she leans closer to the phone. "Where are you?"

The elevator doors open to reveal my floor, punctuating her question. "Almost to my room."

"Ooo, give us a tour."

I know they're just wasting time until I'm behind closed doors to ask me the real questions, but I gladly take the reprieve. Moving slowly, I give them an elaborate tour of the hallway, the door to my room, a detailed viewing of my suite...

When I have nothing left to show them, I drop down onto the bed and squeeze my eyes shut. "Okay, tell me how bad it was."

Suzy scoffs, "Bad? It wasn't bad at all."

I crack one eye open. "I tripped standing still. How is that not bad?"

They both cackle in response, and I groan, "See?!"

Sam shakes her head. "It was hilarious, but it was also cute as hell."

"Cute? Really?" I lift a brow, skeptical.

"Really," Suzy answers. "And when you licked that frosting

28

off your finger..." She fans her face. "I could feel the sexual tension from across the city."

I bolt upright. "Sexual tension? What do you mean?!"

"She means..." Sam smirks. "The off-the-charts, goo-goo eyes you and Chef Mike were throwing at each other."

"But—What—I—" I fall back, slapping a hand over my eyes. "Oh my god, this is so bad!"

"What, why?"

"Because," I whine. "If you can tell that I *like* Michael, then other people watching the show can probably tell too."

"And that would be bad because...?"

I keep my eyes covered. "Because I'm going to look like a pathetic, love-sick loser, and everyone will either pity me or hate me."

"Alice." Suzy's using her stern voice, so I part my fingers to peek out at her.

"What?"

She rolls her eyes. "Did you not hear the part about you two making goo-goo eyes at *each other*?"

Sam nods. "Big time. That man has the hots for you." Then she purses her lips. "So, you're right, most women will probably hate you. But not because they think you're pathetic. They'll hate you because they'll want to be you."

I drop my hand away from my face completely. "What are you talking about?"

Sam taps the screen. "Is this on? Can you hear us?"

"I can hear you talking nonsense! I don't know what you think you saw, but he was not looking at me like"—I wave my hand around—"*that*. I mean, he said my cake was good."

My cousins fan their faces. "What a sweet talker."

I groan. "Shut up. You know that's a compliment coming from him."

"I know what you'd rather have... coming from him."

"Oh my god, you guys are the worst!" I laugh despite myself. "I gotta go."

"Yeah, yeah. Go get your beauty sleep." Suzy blows me a kiss.

"And wear that green skirt tomorrow!" Sam grins.

"Fine." I roll my eyes. "Love you."

They chorus their love back to me as I end the call.

I wonder what they meant by all that sexual tension talk. He can't possibly...

My fingers twitch to search for today's episode, but I really don't want to see myself on camera. Or at least not until the whole thing is done. If I watch it now, I'll for sure hate the way I look on screen, and then I'll be self-conscious about it for the rest of the weekend. So, no watching.

Dropping my phone onto the bed, I decide my best plan of action is going to sleep. I can't make any bad decisions if I'm asleep.

MICHAEL

I spit into the sink and rinse off my toothbrush.
Go to bed.
Just go to bed and go to sleep.

Flipping off the lights as I cross the room, I yank the sheets back and drop onto the mattress.

Close your eyes.

I stare up at the ceiling, thinking back over the information I just read on the *Second Bite* website.

Alice Hatter lives in Minneapolis, works in tech, and is thirty years old.

Thirty to my forty-five.

Just go to sleep, you pervy fuck!

My hand slaps down on my nightstand, picking up my phone.

It only takes a few taps to find what I'm looking for. A screenshot of Alice sucking that damn frosting off her finger.

You're a disgusting man.

But even my inner voice can't stop my body's reaction to Alice. To the sight of her lips circled around the tip of her finger. The invitation in her eyes. The way her small hand felt in my larger, rough one.

Keeping my eyes on the screen, my free hand shoves down the waistband of my pajama pants.

This is fucked up.

I grit my teeth as my palm connects with my dick.

Mine isn't the hand I want to feel. I want her soft, warm fingers wrapped around my hard, hot length.

I want her wide green eyes blinking up at me.

My hand pumps.

I want her kneeling before me, lips parted, pretty pink tongue peeking out to lap at the glaze dripping from my cock.

My grip tightens.

I want to grip her glossy golden hair and hold her still while I shove my dick deep into her willing mouth, bumping against the back of her throat. I want to see the wide-eyed look of surprise when she realizes just how deep she can take me. Just how much of me she can swallow.

A loud groan rips from my chest as I give a final stroke, my release coating my stomach.

ALICE

Flipping onto my stomach, I yell into my pillow.

My limbs flail, and I let out as much frustration as I can.

But it's not enough.

With my eyes squeezed shut, I boost myself up onto my knees, my shoulders still on the mattress. Then, shifting my weight, I reach a hand down between my legs.

Wet. I'm soaking wet just from reliving the few embarrassing interactions I had with Michael in my mind.

Good god, what would it be like to have his hands on me?

To feel *his* hand sliding down my belly.

To feel *his* fingers work their way into my panties.

To feel *his* fingers brush against the slickness of my sex.

Would he gasp? Groan? Growl?

Would he tease me? Running his fingers up and down my slit?

Or would he plunge in, stretching me around his thick fingers?

Would he play with my clit while whispering dirty things to me?

His sexy lips brushing against my skin.

His breath feathering across my neck.

My body seizes with the first waves of an orgasm, my pussy clenching around nothing.

With thoughts of Michael dancing in my mind, I collapse back onto the mattress, where sleep finally takes me.

ALICE

"Thirty minutes left!"

My heartbeat flutters at Joey's announcement. But I can't allow myself to lose focus. And no matter how much I want to open that freezer door, I won't. I need every extra second on the clock for my ice cream to set, or else it'll never hold its shape.

Taking a deep breath to steady my hands, I go back to my piping.

So far, everything is going to plan. My dyed-black gingerbread came out of the oven on time, and the pieces are fitting together perfectly to make a cute little top hat.

As slowly as I'm able, I use gold icing to draw a buckle onto the front, completing the hat.

With the eyes and mouth pieces already done, I just have to finish making the fondant carrot, then I can start assembling.

In the freezer is a round springform pan holding my vanilla chai ice cream, filled with a gooey cinnamon center. And then I have another tray cooling in the freezer that's holding my Jell-O, which will serve as the final decoration.

If it all goes to plan, the ice cream will freeze solid. When I take it out of the pan, I'll cut a thin slice off one side so the circle will stand upright. Then, I'll decorate the vertical surface with button eyes, a carrot nose, and coal bricks for a mouth to make a classic snowman. And I'll complete the look with a gingerbread top hat and a red Jell-O scarf.

It took me forever to figure out how to make the scarf. But by using one of those snaking "only edges" brownie pans, I've been able to make a long continuous piece of Jell-O that makes a decent approximation of a scarf. And if I have time, I'll add some white frosting stripes over the shiny red surface. But that'll depend—

"Ten minutes left!"

My head jerks up to the large clock at the front of the room.

How did so much time pass already?!

My fingers tremble as I press in the final groove on my little carrot, then set it aside.

"Okay," I say under my breath. "Just like you practiced."

With a spot ready on my island for the assembly, I hurry over to my freezer and yank open the door.

I'm so focused on getting my ice cream out that I don't notice anything is wrong until it's in my hands. But when I look down, I almost scream.

Instead of seeing a smooth white surface dotted with flecks of chai, I'm staring down at a homicide scene.

"Oh no," I whisper.

Bright red splotches cover the entirety of my cake.

My eyes fly to the shelf above where I'd put the ice cream, and I fight down the urge to vomit.

I don't know how it happened, but the Jell-O tray must've sprung a leak. Or I bumped it when I put it in. Or something...

"Oh no," I repeat.

Whatever happened, it looks like the entire Jell-O mixture spilled into my ice cream.

I swallow against my rising panic as the din of the room

comes back to me, and I realize I'm out of time. Speed is the only thing that can help me now.

Leaving the cursed Jell-O tray in the freezer, I rush over to my counter and free the ice cream from the spring mold.

I'll just slice off the top layer, and it'll just be a skinny snowman.

Pulling away the springform sides, my spirits sink. It's not just a thin layer that's been ruined. The red has seeped farther into the cake than I thought.

Okay, just flip it over. Hide the disaster. The snowman doesn't need to stand up.

Grabbing a serving platter, I quickly flip the ice cream cake onto the new plate.

And decide I want to die.

Somehow the Jell-O melted rivulets all the way through the cake.

Why did I put the ice cream on the lower shelf!?

I want to slap myself in the face. But I can't. I need to present something. And I need to ignore the camera person who just moved closer to stand beside me.

Working as fast as I can, I stick with the original plan. If it's going to be a disgusting mess, then it's going to be a standing mess. And I need the decorations to be as good as possible.

My movements are frantic, and my hands are shaking so bad they look blurry.

"One minute left!"

I let out a squeal as I shove the last eye into the softening surface of the ice cream.

I look up at the camera guy with pleading eyes, hoping he'll tell me it looks great. But he's biting down on his lip. Hard. Trying not to laugh.

It's a fucking disaster.

Joey calls time, and I step back from my twisted creation.

"Alright, contestants"—Joey claps his hands—"to mix it up, we're going in the opposite order from yesterday."

All gazes turn to land on me.

With every step the judges take, my face pales a shade, until I'm sure I look just as dead as my snowman.

When the group stops in front of me, I can't even look at Michael.

He hardly said a word to me earlier when they came around to hear my plan. And now... well now, I'm more embarrassed than I've ever been in my life and the judgment hasn't even started.

"Alice, tell us about your..." Joey's cheerful voice trails off as he takes in the sight before us.

"Oh, dear." Pamela's sentiment says it all.

As a collective, we all stand and stare at the atrocity of a snowman that I created.

The round circular face isn't a pretty speckled white. It's a jagged, splotchy mess of mottled snow flesh with streaks of gore. The button eyes and coal mouth look menacing and evil. And the black top hat is the literal icing on top of my monstrous creation.

And as we all watch, the carrot nose falls off the snowman's face and the gooey cinnamon filling oozes out of the newly formed hole.

"Oh no," I croak.

MICHAEL

*M*y mouth opens, but for the first time in the history of the show, I'm speechless.

The thing in front of me is... bad. Like really fucking bad. So bad I'm struggling for words to describe its badness.

We all stand still for a moment.

"It's—" Pamela starts.

And when she trails off, I finish. "An abomination."

My eyes are glued to the demonic snowman, the melting process making it more horrific with each passing second, so I miss whatever expression crosses Alice's face at my proclamation. But when I look up, she's looking down. Her hands are twined in the green fabric of her skirt, and I can see the tension in her features.

Joey clears his throat. "Alice, would you walk us through your, uh, creation?"

Alice's hands twist in her skirt more, pulling the top band down just a fraction of an inch.

The off-white silk blouse she's wearing is tucked into her waistband, and my mind wanders to thoughts of undressing her.

How much tugging on that skirt would it take to expose a strip of flesh around her midriff?

Is she wearing stockings?

What would it be like to have my face up under her skirt?

Her lyrical voice floats into my awareness, and I hear her say something about *gingerbread* and *chai* and *cinnamon.*

Pamela steps closer to me to examine Alice's ice cream, and it snaps me out of my daydream.

Shifting my stance, I adjust the two empty plates in front of me and pick up the knife.

The mini top hat slowly slides off the snowman's head, plopping down onto the counter—leaving a trail of pinkish slime in its wake.

"I'm so sorry." Alice's whisper has my eyes snapping back up to her face.

She looks pale, and I want to reassure her, tell her it's all gonna be okay. But when I look back down at the melting mess, I know there's no reassurance to be had.

With the tip of my knife, I press against the snowman's forehead, tipping him back until he flops down onto the plate with a wet slap.

"It'll be easier to cut this way," I explain as I carve out two slices.

With both plates ready, I'm deciding where to take my first bite from when Pamela asks, "What's the red stuff?"

Yeah, good question. What is *the red stuff?*

Alice murmurs a reply, but I don't catch it.

"A little louder, please?" Joey coaxes.

His tone is too friendly. Too familiar. And I want to shove my fork into his arm.

Instead, I fill my fork and shove it into my mouth.

"It's Jell-O."

Alice's sentence takes a second for my brain to compute.

And at that same time, my taste buds start cataloging the flavors.

Warm vanilla and sweetness. Cardamom, ginger, and cloves of chai. Cinnamon. A tangy flavor reminiscent of processed fruit.

My mouth automatically opens, and my body bends forward, letting the un-swallowed portion fall out and onto my plate.

There are a few gasps. A few chuckles. But all I can do is gape at the woman across from me.

"What the hell was that?" I point at the mangled corpse between us. "Explain."

Alice's eyes move everywhere except to meet mine. And I know I'm being a dick, but seriously, that was *bad*.

"Oh, come now." Pamela scoops up a forkful. "It can't be that bad."

I spare her a quick glance. "It's the worst thing I've ever eaten."

A small, distressed sound squeaks out of Alice, and when I look back, I see that her shoulders have hunched forward, and her chin has tipped down even farther.

"T-the Jell-O was supposed to be a scarf." Alice's words are shaky but loud enough to be heard. "Something happened to the tray in the freezer, and it spilled into my ice cream cake." Her hands tug at her skirt some more. "It was just supposed to lay around the base of the cake as a decoration. Not..." She lifts a shoulder. *Not melt into this catastrophe.*

"What flavor is it?" I ask, not easing my tone. I can't. This is the ugliest thing that's ever been presented, and it tastes just as bad. And if I don't react with my usual hard-ass personality, then I'll be accused of playing favorites.

"It's, um, it's tropical punch."

I stare at her, briefly forgetting that this is the woman I plan to make mine, and shake my head. "Tropical punch? What were

41

you thinking? Even if your little scarf plan had worked, it'd still be terrible."

She's nodding her head, but I can't see her face anymore—it's turned down so far. "I'm sorry, Michael."

She whispers it, but it hits me the same as if she'd shouted.

Michael.

The way she said my name was the strongest sort of aphrodisiac.

Pamela covers her startled noise with a cough, knowing damn well that contestants aren't supposed to call me that.

Every muscle in Alice's lush body tenses, and I know she's realized her mistake.

I want to tell her it's okay. That she can call me Michael, hell she can call me anything if she'll just lift her head and let me see her sparkling green eyes.

But again, I can't do any of the things I want to do. So I'm left with no choice but to be my brutally honest self.

"Each flavor on the plate needs to be intentional." I slide the plate away from me. "It all needs to balance and complement. If you'd done that, it wouldn't matter that your presentation was a disgusting mess, the flavors could've saved you. But now we're left with an inedible pile of wasted ingredients."

Alice doesn't answer; she just keeps nodding her head.

Pamela sets her fork down without using it and picks up the little gingerbread hat. "The execution might've failed, but the idea was very clever. Had it turned out, I trust the snowman would've been charming." She breaks off a piece of hat that hasn't been touched by the ice cream and hands me half.

With my eyes on the top of Alice's head, fingers twitching to touch her shiny hair, I put the gingerbread in my mouth.

It's flavorful. The texture is nice. It's a good cookie.

"Very nice." Pamela smiles before I can say anything. "You did a good job with the gingerbread."

"Thank you." Alice's voice cracks.

Aw, fuck.

I know I was being tough but—

One of Alice's hands releases its death grip on her skirt, and she reaches up to brush across her cheek.

My chest tightens.

Is she—

Alice sniffles.

And a jolt of pain shoots down my spine.

She's crying.

My Alice.

My beautiful Christmas Miracle is crying.

And I'm the cause.

Balling my hands into fists, I resist the urge to use my discarded fork to pry my own heart out of my chest as an apology.

But of course, I can't do that. I can't even tell her I'm sorry. I can only step back with the rest of the crew and pretend that walking away isn't tearing me apart inside.

ALICE

*A*nother drip of reddish water splashes onto my shirt, and I have to press my lips together to stop the whimper that wants to come out.

Michael spit out my cake.

He said it was an abomination.

Terrible.

The worst thing he's ever eaten.

An inedible mess.

I sniff and wring out the cloth into a second bowl before dunking it back into the first one filled with warm, soapy water.

Centering myself, I pull in a breath and scrub at another frozen Jell-O spot in the freezer.

I had to stay standing beside my horrendous dessert while the judges went to the other three contestants. But I couldn't repeat a single thing that was said about the other ice cream desserts. My ears were too full of shame to hear anything, and my cloudy gaze stayed rooted to the floor.

No matter what happens tomorrow, I'm not winning. Not unless every other person commits a heinous crime tonight, ends up in jail, and therefore drops out of the competition.

"Uh, ma'am, you don't have to do that," a voice states from somewhere behind me.

"I know." I try to steady my voice. "But it's my fault."

They called a wrap on the episode a few minutes ago, but I couldn't in good conscience leave and make some other poor soul clean this up. Plus, if I'm being honest, I couldn't face the other contestants. They'll all walk back to the rooms together, just like yesterday, and talk about dinner and what time to meet in the restaurant. And I just can't. I can't do small talk. I can't do dinner. I can't just laugh it off and pretend I'm okay.

It's not even about losing. Without my disaster today, there was only ever a slim chance of me walking away a winner, getting the prestige and several thousand dollars. I mean, the money would be great. It wouldn't keep me from losing my apartment or get me that dream bakery, but it would've helped my situation.

But that's only salt in the wound, or should the saying be *fruit punch in the ice cream?*

I snort, but my tiny attempt at a laugh morphs into a tiny sob, and I clap my free hand over my mouth.

Just finish cleaning this up, then you can go to your room.

Just make it through the next ten minutes.

Just pretend you didn't embarrass yourself in front of the man you've loved for years.

I press my hand down harder, a pair of tears rolling down my cheeks.

You're almost done.

I scrub at the last frozen puddle, pushing all my disappointment into the freezer, when a warm palm settles against my lower back. The heat seeping through my clothing, just above the waistband of my skirt.

"Don't cry." Michael's deep voice brushes against my ear. "It's just dessert."

45

Emotion swamps me, and instead of stopping my tears, his words send them flowing down my cheeks.

Michael is here.

Touching me. Comforting me.

Telling me it's just dessert.

My chest hitches.

Dessert is his whole life.

"Please don't cry, Baby Cakes." The pressure of his hand on my back increases. "I can't take you crying."

MICHAEL

She shudders under my hand, and I want to punch myself in the face.

You're making it worse.

You came over here to try and comfort her. But now she's crying more.

Movement in my peripheral has me shifting my gaze from the side of Alice's pretty face to the crew member standing a few feet away. Camera in his hand. Lens aimed at us.

Years in the entertainment industry keep me from reacting.

Yanking my hand away from Alice, or snapping at him to stop recording, would only amplify the situation. So instead, I turn back to Alice and raise my voice to its normal volume, sure the microphone on the camera will pick it up.

"Thank you for cleaning. You can go now."

There's another sniffle, then she turns—away from me and away from the camera—and hurries off set.

Ignoring the camera myself, I shut the freezer and walk casually in the other direction. Pretending that every inch of me isn't clawing to chase her down and beg for her forgiveness.

ALICE

I click off the bedside lamp, wanting to look out at the night sky over the city rather than stare at my reflection.

I know what I look like. Skirt on, shoes off. Thin camisole on, silk shirt and bra off. Hair messy from sulking on the bed. But enough is enough. I can only wallow in self-pity for so long. And while I wait for room service to bring up my dinner, I'm going to enjoy watching the big fluffy snowflakes fall from the sky.

Christmas Eve is the day after tomorrow. And gloomy mood or not, I love Christmas. I love the sparkly lights, the traditions, the food. And even though tomorrow is the last day of the competition—that I'm surely going to lose—it's also another day that I get to be in the same room as Michael Kesso.

Michael. Ugh, I'm not going to think about how I said his name out loud.

Pressing my palms to the glass, I remember the feel of his hand on my back.

He was so close to me. Talking to me like he cared.

Then he ruined it with his comment about cleaning, shat-

48

tering my confidence all over again. But my cousins texted to tell me about the last clip of the show. How there was still one camera running while the credits ran. Probably just meant to pan around the set, but then he zeroed in on the scene Michael and I were making in front of my freezer. Zooming in on us, focusing on where Michael's hand was against my lower back.

And with that explanation, Michael's change in tone made sense. He'd gotten caught being nice to me. And that wasn't good.

I sigh, and my exhale fogs the glass.

It's just dessert.

Using my fingertip, I trace M + A into the condensation on the window, and feel a small smirk start to form.

If only.

A knock at the door pulls me away from my musing, and I cross the room.

I debate finding something to pull on over my revealing top, but I'm just going to take the tray of food from the server and scurry back into hiding, so I don't bother.

Without looking through the peephole, I open the door and smile.

Except the man standing in front of me isn't holding my dinner. And he's no server.

"Alice, I'm sorry. I..." Michael's voice trails off.

Michael's voice!

MICHAEL

*M*y eyes scan the bar for a certain head of wild blonde curls, but she's not here.

I clench my hands and take a seat at the bar.

Maybe she's on her way down.

It's not like I can really talk to her when she gets here anyway. I already crossed a line with how close I got to her earlier. Giving her more attention now would only throw out extra red flags.

The bartender stops in front of me long enough to take my order, and I keep my eyes on the entrance until he returns with my drink. Straight bourbon.

Sounds of chatter mixed with laughs drift over me from the crowded tables. I look around one more time, making sure I didn't miss Alice. But I didn't.

Touching her was a bad idea.

Getting close enough to smell the sugar cookie scent of her hair was an even worse idea.

I take a sip of my drink, and when I lower it from my lips, I watch a drip of liquid trace a path down the glass, causing images of Alice's tear-stained face to fill my mind.

If she's not here, she's in her room. Probably feeling terrible. Possibly crying. And I can't let her go the rest of the night thinking bad thoughts about herself. I just fucking can't.

Without giving myself a chance to overthink it, I lift the drink back to my mouth and down the rest.

Leaving a bill under my empty glass, I stride away from the noise and exit the bar.

I pull my phone out of my pocket, intending to call my manager and have him get Alice's room number, but decide that will probably take forever.

Instead, I cut across the large lobby and aim for the woman working behind the front desk.

She spots me, and I can tell the moment she recognizes me. *Perfect.*

"Good evening, sir." She beams.

"Evening." I force a friendly smile on my face. "One of the contestants on my show left her phone at the table." I hold up my phone, the plain black case universal enough for anyone to own. "Would you be able to tell me which room Alice Hatter is in? I'll just drop it off on my way up."

"Oh, um..." She hesitates, looking torn.

I know this is against the rules. And I'm aware it makes me a total asshole to use my celebrity status to get her to break the rules, but I'm desperate. And I'm not going to be able to sleep until I've apologized to Alice for my harsh words earlier. Yes, her creation was horrendous, but it was also clever, and I owe her at least one nice compliment.

"She wasn't feeling well, so I figured I'd offer to bring it up rather than making her come back down. But if you can't..." I shrug, knowing that I'm famous for being a bit of a dick.

The woman makes a sympathetic face before glancing around. Seeing that no one is around to overhear, she clicks a few times on her keyboard before looking up. "She's in 612."

"Thank you." I tip my chin as I step back.

612. I let the number sear itself into my brain as I move toward the elevators.

I run over my apology in my mind, discarding options as soon as I come up with them.

I'm sorry I called your ice cream the worst thing I've ever tasted.

Sorry I spit it out in front of the whole world.

I step into the empty elevator cab and jab my finger against the 6.

I'm sorry for making you cry. I know you don't know a thing about me, but I'm pretty sure I'm half in love with you and I'd rather die than make you cry again.

Sorry I didn't just eat the whole disgusting cake. Because I will, if it'll make you smile.

The elevator stops, and I step off onto Alice's floor.

Taking a few deep breaths to slow my suddenly racing heart, I stop in front of door 612.

No hesitating.

You didn't get to where you are by hesitating.

I knock.

And then I wait a thousand years for the door to swing open.

Not wanting her to slam the door in my face, I jump right into it.

"Alice, I'm sorry. I..." The rest of my sentence dies in my throat.

Holy Mrs. Claus, my Christmas wish just came true.

Alice is standing before me, eyes wide, hair mussed as if she'd just been well fucked. That bright green skirt dancing around her knees and... I have to work to swallow so I don't drool down my chin. *Sweet snowballs, her tits are amazing.*

I'm not sure if what she's wearing can even be called a shirt. It's so thin. And it looks so soft. And it's doing absolutely nothing to hide her perfectly plump breasts.

I was just coming up to apologize, but if I make it out of here without sucking one of those nipples into my mouth, it'll be a damn miracle.

ALICE

*T*he man of my dreams is standing in front of me, in real life, in front of *my* hotel room. And he's staring at my boobs.

My hands twitch, and I know I should cross my arms over my chest. Or step back and swing the door shut. But I'm stuck in place, shock locking my muscles.

"I, uh..." He pauses before he glances back up to meet my eyes. "I wanted to apologize."

"Apologize?" I'm so stunned by his presence that I'd almost forgotten about the humiliating afternoon.

"Yes, apologize." He seems to shake himself off. "I was cruel, and you—"

His words cut off at the sound of the elevator door dinging open. Voices drift down the hallway, and it only takes one laugh for us to both recognize it as Joey's.

"Shit," Michael growls, taking a step toward me, closing the distance between us.

Our bodies collide, my breasts pressed into the hard planes of his chest. But Michael doesn't stop. He circles an arm around my back, and in one swift move, he lifts me, steps forward—propelling me back into the room—and kicks the door shut.

The sound of our heavy breaths fill the entryway of my room, drowning out any voices that might still be in the hallway.

Ohmygod, ohmygod, ohmygod.

Michael is in my room.

His arm is around me.

He can probably feel my nipples through his shirt.

His face is so close to mine.

The room is dark, making the scene feel even more provocative than it is. And I try to listen to the reasonable part of my brain, which is telling me that he's just trying to avoid us getting caught together. Since he's a judge and I'm a competitor. And he's just here to apologize.

That's what he said.

Michael's chest expands on a large inhale, and his dark eyes search mine.

"Fuck it," he growls, a brief moment before his mouth closes on mine.

Time. Stops.

Warm lips press against my own.

Michael Kesso is kissing me.

Me!

I gasp when my mind finally catches up to what's happening, and Michael takes full advantage, plunging his tongue between my lips.

Bolts of sensation zip through my body, sparking against every inch of exposed skin, and I stop thinking altogether.

With a moan, I lean into him, kissing him back.

One large palm cups the side of my face.

His hand feels so warm against my flushed cheek. Thick fingers brushing gently over that sensitive spot in front of my ear, the pads rough from years of use in the kitchen.

I squeeze my eyes closed tighter. Afraid that if I look too closely, I'll find this is all a dream.

A sound moves through Michael's chest, and my hands reach out, seeking the vibration.

His body is already against mine, but I grip at his sides, my fingers clutching at the smooth material of his shirt, tugging him to me.

I need him closer.

I need more of him touching more of me.

Like he heard my thoughts, Michael's arm around my back tightens as he rotates us.

Letting go of his shirt, I reach my arms up around his neck, letting him maneuver our bodies wherever he wants.

I still don't understand what's happening. But I'm not gonna question it.

Not yet.

If he dropped me on the bed right now and asked to have sex, I'd willingly light my clothes on fire if it expedited the activity.

"Alice." He murmurs my name against my lips.

My back bumps against the wall, making my eyes pop open.

Michael's gaze is staring back at me.

"I'm so sorry, Baby Cakes," he whispers, brushing his lips over mine again. "Forgive me."

Before I can answer, he's crushing his mouth back to mine. And I feel like I can taste his apology. It's bourbon and ginger mixed with sincerity.

His hands tangle in my hair, drawing my head back, breaking our kiss.

Michael runs his mouth across my cheek, down my neck.

"Tell me you understand," Michael rasps against my fluttering pulse. "Tell me you forgive me."

"I forgive you." My voice is hardly recognizable. Or maybe it's just the lust buzzing through my body, blurring my senses.

He groans, rolling his body against mine, and I finally take notice of the stiffness pressing into my belly.

He does it again, and this time my groan mingles with his.

"Mi—" I catch myself.

He tugs on my hair. "Say it."

My breath catches.

"Say it, Alice. Say my name."

"Michael." It's barely a breath, but I know he hears it because suddenly, the full weight of his body leans into mine. Pinning me in place.

The sensation of having Michael so close is vibrant. Decadent. Precious. It's like a string of lights has been wrapped around me and plugged in, with no regard for safety. Like Christmas morning served up as a kiss in a man-sized package.

"Let me taste your tits."

His words snap me back to the moment.

"Taste my—?"

"Please," he begs against my throat. "Let me taste them. Say yes."

My breasts are already throbbing, with an echoing response between my legs.

The hands in my hair release, sliding down the bare skin of my neck… my shoulders… to my sides.

His palms are warm against my ribs, his thumbs barely an inch below the bottom swell of my breasts.

My tits.

I nod.

His thumbs shift. "Use your words, Baby Cakes."

"Yes, Michael."

He drops his face until his forehead hits that spot between my neck and shoulder.

"Yes, what?" It sounds like the words were dragged out of him.

My face flames before I even say the words. "Yes. Please, Michael, will you suck on my tits?"

"Jesus."

The way he says the word makes me feel like I should cross myself. Not that I'd even know how.

A loud rip fills the space a moment before cool air hits my bare skin.

"Fuck, Baby." Michael's tone is reverent as he takes a tit in each hand. "Goddamn perfection."

I've always been a little self-conscious of my boobs. A touch too large. Not perky enough. Nipples a little too big.

But the look on Michael's face matches the sound of his voice. And the sight of his big hands supporting my breasts has me feeling like the most desirable woman in the world.

I open my mouth to say something, but then *his* mouth opens... and closes over one peak.

Even knowing that it was coming, I still startle, nearly choking on my indrawn breath.

This isn't real.

A tongue laps at my stiff nipple.

This seriously can't be real.

His hands knead and squeeze.

His teeth scrape and bite.

His mouth sucks and licks.

And I die, just a bit.

MICHAEL

The sounds coming out of Alice go straight to my dick, and I close my teeth on her soft, supple skin.

She's perfect. Absolutely, undeniably, fucking perfect.

And I need more.

So I tell her.

"I need more, Baby. Let me have more."

Alice drops her head back against the wall, her hands locked in a death grip on my shoulders, bunching the fabric of my shirt.

"Take more," she sobs. "Take whatever you want."

Images of our life together flash through my mind.

Diamond rings. A white dress. Sunny beaches. Tiny babies.

She doesn't realize what she's offering. What I'm willing to take.

But that comes later.

That's what I'll claim after.

I lower myself to my knees.

Letting go of her glorious tits, I drag my hands down her sides. Down her hips... the length of her legs... until I reach the bottom hem of her skirt.

Alice tips her head forward to look down at me. "What are you doing?"

"I didn't get enough to eat earlier." I feel the side of my mouth pull up in a smirk. "Why go hungry when there's a snack right here?"

"S-snack?"

Her face flames red, and my smirk grows into a grin. "Lift your skirt for me, Sweetness."

As she stares, I reach down and grab one of her ankles.

"What—"

Before she can ask again, I lift her foot off the ground and slide my grip up her leg, still lifting. I don't stop until I've put her knee over my shoulder.

Her skirt drapes over her thigh, and I turn my head so I can give her a gentle nip on the inside of her knee. "Skirt."

At my reminder, Alice reaches down and—with shaking fingers—she bunches the material, higher and higher, until I can see the holly-berry-red panties she's been hiding underneath.

Mother of Christmas, this is a sight worth remembering.

I lean in, touching the tip of my nose to the soft red fabric, and press a chaste kiss against her panties.

She sways.

I pull back just enough to look up at her.

"Lean back against the wall."

She just blinks at me, so I say it again.

"Lean against the wall, Alice."

She does as she's told.

"Arms out."

"Arms?" she repeats.

I nod. "Spread your arms against the wall, Baby. For balance."

Her eyes are slightly glazed over, but she takes a second to tuck her skirt up into her waistband before she spreads her arms out, her hands pressing into the wall.

"Good girl," I growl.

Then, making sure to keep us both steady, I hoist her other leg up and over my shoulder until she's suspended in the air, straddling my face.

Alice lets out a small shriek, and I hear something small drop to the carpet next to me, but I can't focus on anything beyond the sight in front of me. Specifically, the dark, damp spot on her pretty little panties.

"Are you wet for me, Sweetness?"

She shifts and moans, lowering her hands from the wall to clutch my hair.

I should go slow. I should lay her on the bed, not pin her to the wall. But I can't hold back. Not for a single second longer.

I hook my arms up around her legs, securing her in place, with my hands gripping the inside of her thighs. Inches away from her pussy.

Shifting closer, I hook one finger around the edge of her panties and pull them to the side. Revealing her glistening pink slit.

Her legs tense, trying to close.

But they can't. Because I'm here. And I'm not leaving until she comes.

"Delicious," I groan, leaning in.

ALICE

*a*ir hits my exposed pussy, and I tighten my grip on Michael's hair.

This is happening.

I'm sitting on his shoulders. His face is inches from my vagina. And ohmygod, this is happening!

My eyes dart over to see my silver dollar roll out of sight under the bed.

I was starting to doubt that talisman and the need to keep it in my pocket, but clearly, it works.

"Delicious."

My gaze moves back to Michael at the same moment a warm tongue licks against my entrance.

"Holy—" I suck in a breath as he laps at me. Again and again. "Oh god. Oh my god."

I tilt my hips, offering him more.

"Say my name," he grits out before licking again. "Tell me how it feels." He punctuates his statement by flicking his tongue against my clit.

"Michael. Michael!" I rock my hips against his face. "It feels so good. You feel so good."

His response is lost to me as the vibrations of his words travel through my core, straight into my wildly beating heart.

Hanging on for dear life, I close my eyes and arch into his mouth.

I don't question his level of talent. I just enjoy it.

I enjoy the feeling of his lips on my clit. His tongue pushing into my entrance. His moans against my flesh.

One of the arms he has holding me in place shifts away, and I hook my feet together behind his back, not wanting to tip over.

I can't fall off now. Not when I'm so close.

The suction against my clit increases.

"Michael!" I cry out, the first tremors of release rolling up my spine.

His tongue curls around my bundle of nerves, and just when I think I can't take anymore, two fingers press deep inside of me.

And I explode.

MICHAEL

*H*er pussy convulses around my fingers, nearly sending me over the edge with her.

Alice shakes against me, her wetness practically dripping down my hand.

I want her.

I want to take her.

Withdrawing my hand, I help lower her off my shoulders until she's standing on her own two feet.

Leaning back, I look up at her.

Shirt torn down the front, heaving tits on display.

Skirt tucked up, exposing her panties and glossy slit.

Face flushed from an orgasm that *I* gave her.

She looks completely satisfied.

But then the shine in her eyes reminds me why I came up here.

I came here to apologize. To tell her I'm sorry for making her cry *on my show.* The show that she's a contestant on.

Fuck.

Unaware of my spiraling thoughts, Alice looks down at my lap. "Do you need to...?"

Yeah, I fucking need to.

But I shake my head.

"I can't." I give my head another shake. "I've done too much already."

Her hands jerk up to her chest, covering herself.

"It's not like that," I try to explain, the sudden hurt in her eyes killing me. I ignore the pain in my knees as I push myself back up to standing. "I don't mean it like that, Alice."

She bites her lip and nods, but she won't look at me.

My phone rings from my pocket.

"Shit," I snap, sure it's my manager. He's the only person who calls me, and he'll keep calling until I answer.

Laughter filters in from the hallway, followed by the slamming of doors, then silence.

This is my chance to slip out of here unnoticed, and I need to take it—before I take *her.*

Feeling a piece of my soul rip free and jump toward Alice, I take a step back.

"This isn't over," I say, hoping she'll believe me. "This just can't happen *right now.* Tell me you understand."

She keeps her head tipped down, but I hear her whisper, "I understand."

Needing one more touch, I re-close the distance between us and press a kiss to her hair. "Sweet dreams, Baby Cakes."

ALICE

he door shuts behind Michael with a soft click, and I swear I feel it in my bones.

What just happened?

With my back still against the wall, I stare at the floor in front of me.

Did he...?

Did we...?

And then did he... just leave?

There's a weird twisting in my chest.

Breathe, Alice. Just take a breath.

My lungs fill, and I close my eyes.

It's all okay. This is all totally okay.

The cool air of the room drifts over my skin, and I'm reminded of my destroyed shirt, the literal proof of what just occurred between us.

In a state of semi-numbness, I shuffle to my suitcase and find my pair of flannel pajamas.

I'm usually a very meticulous person, but instead of carefully removing and folding my dirty clothes, I strip them off and drop them on the floor.

I don't know how to feel about what just happened. I don't even know what part to focus on. The fact that Michael, *my Michael*, came to my hotel room to apologize for being his usual self on his show. The fact he kissed me. The fact he begged my forgiveness, then hoisted my entire weight on his shoulders so he could plant his face in my vagina.

With a shiver, I yank on the pants, then button up the loose-fitting shirt as I replay Michael's words.

I can't.

I've done too much already.

That twisting feeling amplifies until the center of my chest hurts.

It's not like that, he said.

I don't mean it like that, he repeated.

But how else could he mean it? There's not really a nice way to tell someone that giving them an orgasm was a mistake.

Maybe he would've said more, but then he got that phone call. At night. And he seemed determined to answer it.

I know more than I should know about Michael Kesso, but maybe he has a secret girlfriend. Lover. *Dear god*, maybe he has a wife.

I shake my head at the thought.

No. He doesn't have a wife. No way would he be able to do that without the press knowing. Secret short-term girlfriend, maybe. But not something like that.

This isn't over, Alice. This just can't happen right now. Tell me you understand.

I told him that I understood. But I don't. What's not over? The show? Us fooling around? Honestly, I have so little idea about what might be going on in his head, it's alarming. I thought I knew everything there was to know about him.

My inner voice snorts at me. *You didn't know what his kisses tasted like.*

A knock at the door startles me so bad I let out a little scream.

Did he come back?

"Uh, room service," the voice tentatively says from the other side of the door. A voice that is definitely not Michael's.

Surprised I can still feel embarrassed after everything I've been through today, I hurry to the door and take the covered tray from the server. Giving them a bigger tip than I can afford, I hope the extra cash will make up for my frazzled state.

Dropping down onto my bed with my burger on my lap, I think about the last thing Michael said and wonder how many ways I can interpret tonight's encounter before I have to see him again tomorrow.

Sweet dreams, Baby Cakes.

Yeah, right.

ALICE

"... *H*ave four hours, and your time starts now!" Joey calls out from the front of the room, and his declaration is immediately followed by sounds of bowls and pans clanking together as we all scramble to get our final cakes started.

I've spent the whole morning stressing over Michael. Over our kiss, the things we did, the fact that he left...

And I'll admit that I've cried a few more tears over my ice cream Leatherface, knowing that I won't be winning at the end of today.

I've accepted it.

But I'm choosing courage.

I'm going to work as hard as I can today to put something together that's both beautiful and delicious in front of the judges. In front of Michael.

And when I'm finally forced to look at him, rather than avoid his gaze—as I've been doing up until now—I'm going to meet his eyes with a calm smile on my face. I'm going to pretend that there's nothing weird between us and that my heart isn't seizing in my chest.

MICHAEL

"... Four hours, and your time starts now!"
My gaze is locked on Alice as Joey lifts his arms, signaling the beginning of the competition.

The episode may have just officially started, but there's a significant amount of prep time before the cameras start rolling, especially with this live streaming bullshit, and Alice has made sure to avoid my eye since the second she stepped on set. But she hasn't avoided my attention. Not in that fucking outfit.

My hands itch to drag her back to her hotel room to finish what we started. But that's not how this is gonna go, so instead, I keep my hands busy by shoving my sleeves up my arms.

Objectively, this is the most conservative outfit she's worn on the show. But in reality, every single one of her glorious curves is on graphic display.

She's wearing high-waisted red pants that have some sort of big, loopy bow on the back, making her ass look like a literal wrapped present. And her top—I gulp, taking her in for the hundredth time—she's wearing a short-sleeved turtleneck. Reserved-sounding on paper, but it's skin-fucking-tight and made of some sort of shimmery silver material. And *holy jingle bells, I want to sink my teeth into her!*

Last night was… a lot of things. And I regret how I ran out of there, but I don't regret a single second of our encounter.

I should.

I should feel bad about messing around with a contestant. But she's not just a contestant. She's my future. My Alice.

And I do feel bad that she won't be winning today. There's just no way, not after that snowman—but honestly, it's for the best. Because I won't be keeping her a secret. I figure the whole world will know about us by New Year's, so at least this way, there's no way anyone can accuse me of playing favorites.

But after tonight, she won't need that seed money to build a bakery. I'll give her whatever she needs. Whatever she fucking wants, her wildest dreams, it's hers. Alice Hatter will want for nothing.

With half an ear, I listen to Hugh tell us about his cake. Then Brent. Then Mikayla prattles on, batting her lashes, leaning down to point at ingredients, knowing full well her low-cut shirt is gaping for the camera—and for me. But I'm not interested.

And I don't care what my manager says. I don't care if there's already chatter on Twitter about the way I look at Alice, the way I touched her back yesterday when she was crying into her freezer… I'm not going to be "over-friendly" with the other bakers to "counteract the image." Not now. Not ever.

Thinking about where I was when he started calling me last night, I nearly crack a smile. If he had any idea my face was still wet with Alice's release when I answered the phone, he'd probably have a heart attack.

But I don't pay my manager to be my morality police. I pay him to make me money. And I'd bet that ratings are gonna skyrocket when people find out that I found my wife on *Second Bite.* So, if anything, he should be thanking me for my *behavior.*

"Sounds quite ambitious. Good luck!" Pamela bumps me with her hand as she gestures to Mikayla, and I'm sure it's on purpose.

I nod my head. "Use your time wisely."

Mikayla's smile dims a little at my even tone. But I'm not saying it specifically to be a jerk. It's one of my standard lines.

A small voice in the back of my mind tells me that that's probably why it bothers her. She's clearly trying to get my attention beyond her skills as a baker, but I'm just not interested.

I hold out a hand for Pamela to walk ahead of me, and she takes the offer, moving to the final station.

It looks chivalrous, but I'm doing it so I get to stand in the spot directly in front of Alice.

Time's up, Baby Cakes. No more avoiding me.

ALICE

I've been tracking the judges' progress around the room and time it just right so that I'm mixing the wet and dry ingredients for my batter when they approach my table.

I wouldn't have been able to focus on measuring with Michael standing across from me, so I had to finish that part before they got here to stay on schedule, but stirring will give me something to focus on.

"Hello, Alice." Michael's deep voice rolls over my skin, sending a shiver through my body.

"H-Hi," I stammer like a fool.

Pamela gives me a motherly smile. "How're you feeling today?"

Oh good, she's referring to yesterday's disaster.

My cheeks flame to a color that probably matches my pants, and I fight the urge to go shove my head in my unlucky freezer.

I can't stop my eyes from flicking to Michael's, and of course, he's staring right back at me with a knowing smirk on his handsome face.

"It felt good." My eyes widen. "I mean, I feel good." My words come out like a squeak, and I hope everyone just assumes I'm still embarrassed about my catastrophic display yesterday and not that I'm suddenly thinking about Chef Michael's tongue on my clit.

"Glad to hear it," Michael responds as he steps closer to my counter. "Tell me what you're planning to do."

"What I'm planning...?" I repeat, my gaze automatically dropping to his waist.

Michael clears his throat.

My entire body bursts into literal flames.

I evaporate into dust.

And my humiliation is no more.

MICHAEL

CHRIST.

I clear my throat and shift closer to the countertop, blocking Alice's view of the front of my pants and hopefully blocking the cameras from getting a shot of my growing bulge.

I ask her what she's planning, and she looks at my dick.

Fuck me.

I'm planning that too, Sweetness.

Joey snickers at my side, startling Alice. Her whole body jolts, and the bowl of ingredients she's nearly overmixed starts to tip.

Reaching out, I steady the bowl.

Alice closes her eyes for a second. "Sorry."

She takes a breath, and I watch her shoulders visibly relax.

When she opens her eyes, she focuses on Pamela. "Seems I'm still a little rattled."

"That's okay, dear. Happens to the best of us." Pamela pats Alice's arm. "Why don't you take a moment and tell us what you're making today."

Alice nods, biting her lip for a second, before jumping into her explanation. "I'm making a traditional Norwegian cream cake as the base in honor of my grandmother. And for the filling, I'll be using a mixture of lingonberries and cloudberries for an added nod to Scandinavia."

"Ooo." Pamela's eyes widen as she looks at the bowls of produce laid out on the counter. "Are the cloudberries fresh?"

Alice gives her first non-forced smile of the day. "I'm using both fresh and preserved to get the right effect. They can be hard to come by, but I know a guy here in Minnesota who grows them indoors."

My mood darkens. "What—" I stop myself before I get the rest of the question out. Growling *what guy* on air might be a step too far. "What's your plan for the decorations?"

Alice's eyes meet mine. "It's a bit complicated." She shifts, then moves her focus back to Pamela. "I'm going to attempt to make a Christmassy snow globe. The cream cake will be the base. I'm using sugar cookies shaped and decorated like ornaments around the sides of the cake. There'll be a transparent sugar dome over the top, and inside the *globe*, I'll have a kransekake." She glances at the camera and explains, "It's basically a stack of cookies that get smaller as you go up. And with some colored fondant lights, I'll hopefully make it look like a Christmas tree." She sighs. "I might be biting off more than I can chew, but I'll do my best."

The look on her face is a mixture of determination and hope, and I find myself smiling. "I have confidence in you."

Alice's mouth pops open, clearly not expecting me to say that.

When she continues to just blink at me, I'm forced to bite my tongue to prevent myself from telling her to close her mouth or put it to use.

"Sounds marvelous!" Pamela claps her hands together, breaking the moment. "We'll let you get to it."

Reluctantly, I walk away from Alice's table.

ALICE

"*T*hat's halfway! Two hours left!"
  I glance down at my workspace.
I'm on track and feeling good.

"ONE HOUR LEFT!"
  Oh shit!
I'm not on track.

"THIRTY MINUTES!"
  Fuck, fuck, fuck.

"CONTESTANTS, YOU HAVE TEN MINUTES LEFT!"

If I had a single second of spare time, I'd scream curses at Joey for reminding me of the time.

But I'm busy concentrating, trying my best to still my hand while I ice my sugar cookies.

"FIVE MINUTES LEFT!"

Biting on my lip so hard I'm surprised it doesn't bleed, I add the last detail to the last cookie and start pressing them into the side of the round, white-frosted cake.

"TWO MINUTES LEFT!"

The time of reckoning is here. I turn to my extremely fragile sugar dome.

Dear Mr. Kringle, please don't let this break.

I can feel eyes on me as I gently lift the globe from its cooling rack. Blocking out everything around me, I hold my breath and slowly lower it.

"Time's up in three... two..."

The bottom rim of the globe presses into the top of the cake, settling without a crack.

"One! Please step away from your cakes."

ALICE

*W*ith my heart racing, I step away from my masterpiece and absently reach into my pocket, only to remember that I never grabbed my silver dollar off the floor last night.

And just like that, the rush of the competition is mixed with memories of sitting on Michael's face, sending my pulse even higher.

Not now, Alice.

My fingers twitch, but I leave my hand in my pocket. The silver dollar is only worth a dollar, but it was given to me by my grandma and is important to me.

The luck may not have held out for yesterday's cake, but overall, I'm happy with how the last few days have gone. I've done my best. I've done something outside my comfort zone. And I got to meet Michael in person. In a very personal way.

Heaving out another breath, I allow myself to look at Michael for the first time in hours.

He walked around the set, stopping to see everyone's progress once an hour, but I made a point to keep my head down. The camera crew probably hates me, since I'm not engaging well, but I couldn't let myself look at Michael. If I looked at him, I'd want to look at all of him, and I barely finished as it was.

But right now, Michael is preoccupied with Hugh at the table in front of me, so I take the opportunity to look my fill.

This might be the last time I see Michael in person. And if that's the case, I want to soak it in. Between the sight of him and the memories from last night, I should be able to sustain myself until my mid-seventies at least.

Movement at the edge of my vision pulls my attention over, and my face pales.

A third camera person is standing off to the side, her lens aimed right at me.

I drop my gaze to my cake.

Well done, Alice. Way to look like a lovesick puppy until the very end.

A chorus of *good jobs* comes from Hugh's table, and I lift my head, expecting to see them move over to Brent's table, but instead, Joey holds a hand out for the judges to move straight to my station.

Pamela beams. "Wow! This came out stunning!"

"Thank you." I smile back.

My nerves may feel like a bundle of sparking lights, but I'm proud of my effort today. And I'm going to keep my shoulders back.

And I'm going to make eye contact with Michael.

"Yes." Michael's voice sounds like pure sin. "Very beautiful."

I open my mouth to thank him and find his eyes on me instead of the cake, stealing my breath away.

I take a fortifying swallow. "I tried my best."

He nods, then turns his attention to the cake.

My lips press together as I watch him lift the clear sugar dome off the cake, then prepare plates for Pamela and himself.

They each get a slice of cake, an ornament cookie, and one of the rings from the kransekake cookie tree.

I try to watch both of their reactions, but my gaze keeps moving back to Michael's mouth.

He takes several bites of the cake, tasting the layers separately and together.

"Oh my," Pamela exclaims, eyes closing. "This cream cake is absolutely divine."

I pick up the hand towel on my counter so I have something to twist in my grip. "Thank you."

They both set their forks down and move on to the cookies.

Time seems to drag.

Pamela makes little noises of enjoyment as she eats.

"Is there orange in these?" she asks, holding up the sugar cookie.

I nod. "Orange zest and vanilla bean."

"It's brilliant with the cake." She nudges Michael with her elbow. "Don't you agree?"

Michael grunts, moving to taste the next item.

I tip my head toward the partially demolished cookie tree. "I added a little bit of lemon to the kransekake to stick with the fruit and citrus theme. I know they aren't necessarily traditional holiday flavors, but I felt like they fit. And citrus somehow makes a dessert feel lighter. So you don't mind eating it even if you're stuffed," I try to joke but just end up making an awkward gesture.

Both judges finish tasting everything, and I grip the towel tighter.

"Well…" Pamela starts but trails off.

I follow her gaze to Michael's hand as he reaches for the fork he set down earlier.

He isn't…

Michael grabs his fork and scoops up a large bite of the cake. The ambient sound in the room dropping to pure silence.

He is.

My eyes stay glued to his hand as it lifts. Up and up until I'm staring at his mouth, watching his lips part.

Holy shit, he is!

Michael puts the forkful of cake into his mouth for a second bite.

Pride swamps me.

Michael Kesso just took a second bite of my cake.

A Second. Fucking. Bite!

My legs suddenly feel like the Jell-O that turned on me yesterday, and I have to reach out to brace myself against the countertop.

I watch his throat work, expecting him to say something. But instead, he takes another forkful of the cake, and another, until he's finished off the entire slice from his plate.

Pamela chuckles and pats him on the shoulder. "I take it you liked it?"

My gaze finally leaves his mouth to meet his eyes.

He's shaking his head. "Not like. Love."

My heart squeezes.

"Fucking delicious."

One of the camera techs chokes on a laugh, and I hear a gasp come from somewhere else in the room, but I can't even think about the implication of Michael swearing on live TV. I'm too busy being stunned.

I got a Michael Kesso Second Bite.

Tears fill my eyes, but it's for a whole new reason today.

Instead of embarrassment and shame, I'm filled with an immense sense of happiness and pride.

Pamela clicks her tongue. "Language, Mike."

He lifts one shoulder in the most *I don't care* shrug I've ever seen. "Alice is worth the fine."

My mouth goes dry.

Did he just say?

Pamela shakes her head, looking at the ceiling in exasperation. "Alice's *cake*"—she emphasizes the word—"is worth the fine."

Michael doesn't reply, refusing to confirm her statement. He just stares at me as he scrapes the last bit of cream cake off his plate.

When he places the fork in his mouth a final time, closing his lips firmly around the cool metal, an embarrassing sound crawls up my throat.

One of the camera guys moves closer to me, and I watch as Michael's eyes snap to him, pinning him in place with a murderous glare. The camera guy stops, then takes a step back.

"Well." Joey throws his arms out as he comes around the counter to stand beside me. "Talk about a turnaround."

"Thanks," I reply, trying to remember that this is a show and that I need to act like an actual human. "I'm glad I could create something good today."

The corner of Joey's mouth tips up into a smirk right before he drapes an arm around my shoulder.

"Not just good, freaking delicious. Remember?" He winks, but it's not me he's looking at.

Michael's eyes are narrowed at the spot where Joey's body is touching mine, and he slams his fork down on the counter. "We're done here."

Confused but happy, I watch as they all walk across the aisle toward a pouting Mikayla.

ALICE

*M*y nerves are at an all-time high as the four of us stand in a line waiting for the judges to tell us their decision.

I shouldn't be nervous. Even with my "Second Bite" final challenge, I know it's not enough to put me in the running after yesterday's inedible ice cream cake.

Looking around at what's left of the cakes displayed at the front of the room, I wish I'd paid more attention to what the judges said to the other bakers. I think we all did pretty good the first day. I have no clue how anyone did yesterday because I was fighting off sobs instead of listening. And today, I was distracted by Michael, both before and after my judging. So, needless to say, I have no idea who the winner is going to be.

Across the room, Pamela and Michael sit at a small table, discussing the competition and who's gonna win. From years and years of watching this show, I know exactly how their conversation is going. *So and so did well here. Different person did a good job here. And that one person bombed X challenge so bad they're out of the competition altogether.*

Brent bumps my shoulder with his from his spot next to me

in line. "It's been fun baking with you. If you're ever downtown and want to grab a latte, let me know." He winks. "I'll make my boss pay for it."

"Deal." I smile up at him.

Then we give each other a look when Pamela lifts a hand to wave Joey over.

This is it.

They've decided.

Squaring my shoulders, I focus on breathing while trying to keep a serene look on my face.

I did it.

I came onto Second Bite. I finished every challenge. I got the only Second Bite of the weekend. And tomorrow is Christmas Eve, the beginning of my favorite holiday.

With measured steps, the judges and Joey come to stand in front of our little lineup.

"You all did an amazing job over these past three days. There were some big highs and some low lows." He smirks at me, and everyone chuckles.

I guess we're joking about that now. Cool.

Joey takes a deep breath. "But unfortunately, only one of you can be champion of the *Second Bite Holiday Special.*" He pauses for dramatic effect, and I force my gaze to stay on him. "And it's my great pleasure to tell you the winner is…" His eyes catch on each of us before they stop on the beautiful woman at the other end of the row from me. "Congratulations, Mikayla!"

MICHAEL

*M*y eyes stay locked on Alice as Joey announces the winner.

I hate that it's not Alice.

I hate that I have to stand here and watch her lose.

And I hate that there's nothing I can do about it.

The thought of my girl feeling even the smallest amount of heartache makes me want to rip this entire set down.

But as soon as this is over, as soon as we do all the post-challenge interviews, I'm going to pull Alice aside and tell her she's mine.

I just need to be patient for a few more hours.

"FINE!" I snap, cutting off my manager. "Just do what I asked, and I'll make the flight tomorrow morning work."

Not waiting for an answer, I hang up the call and rub a hand down my face.

Usually this wrap-up process is quicker, but since it's all live, they had to do the interviews one at a time, talking to each contestant, talking to each judge… Then getting all the bullshit handshake photos for promos. It's been draining. And a producer somewhere must've said something to someone, since not once was I put anywhere near Alice, which only infuriated me even more.

But we're officially done now. And I'm done waiting.

I'm stomping back into the room from where I took my call in the hallway when Pamela stops me.

"Want to join me for a drink? I'm going out with some of the crew to this historic speakeasy in the basement of a place called The Syndicate Hotel. I've heard it has a shady history." She widens her eyes, and I know that's just the sort of place she'd love.

"No, sorry," I tell her.

"Are you sure?"

"Thanks, but I'm sure." I glance around. "I need to find Alice."

"Oh." Pamela touches her hand to her chest. "She left a while ago."

"What?"

"I thought you saw. They did her interview first and had her leave not long after."

"Shit!" I clench my fists, pissed at myself for missing that.

Pamela's expression softens. "I'm sure you'll find her."

"Oh, I'll find her," I growl before turning and striding out of the room.

In a matter of minutes, I'm getting off the elevator on the sixth floor of the hotel.

The entirety of my game plan consists of shredding those fucking red pants and tossing her on the mattress. But that plan dies an agonizing death when I see that her hotel door is currently propped open with a cleaning cart.

"No, no, no," I mutter to myself as I reach her room.

Stepping past the cart, I startle a housekeeper who's carrying a bundle of towels out of the bathroom.

"Oh, hello." She smiles, and I can tell she recognizes me.

Calming my roaring nerves, I force a smile onto my face. "Sorry to bother you, but did the woman in this room check out already?"

Everyone got their hotel room booked through tonight. Even knowing tomorrow is Christmas Eve, I hadn't considered the fact that she might leave early.

The woman nods. "I got the call on my walkie about an hour ago that the room was clear."

"Dammit," I sigh, letting my eyes flick over the spot where I kneeled last night.

I start to turn, but the housekeeper stops me. "If you know her…" She trails off as she drops the towels into the basket on her cart and lifts something off the top shelf. "I found this just under the bed." She holds the large silver coin out to me. "I don't think it was meant to be a tip since she left cash on the end table. So I'm thinking maybe she dropped it."

My fingers close around the coin, and I'm soothed by the weight of holding something that belongs to Alice. "Thank you. I'll make sure she gets it."

MICHAEL

*C*ursing under my breath, I lift my hand and knock on the hollow-sounding door.

I can't believe she lives here. My Alice. My world. Living in a dangerous, unsecured building like this... no. Not now. Not ever.

I knock again, louder.

It took me way too long to get her address out of my manager. Strictly speaking, he probably broke some sort of law giving it to me. But he knows the deal. If I don't find Alice, I don't go to Canada. Simple as that.

But now I'm here, and she's not answering.

"Alice!" I shout, pounding my fist on the door. There's no way she can't hear me. She could probably hear my heartbeat through this shitty door.

The door across the hall opens.

"Hey man, you just missed her," a sleepy—or stoned—voice says to me.

I turn around, finding my anger torn between the fact that I missed her and that her neighbor looks like he belongs on a professional football team.

Needing the information, I tamp down my jealous irritation. "Do you know when she'll be back?"

He shakes his head. "Nah, I mean you *missed* her. Alice moved out."

My head jerks back as if the man just struck me. "She moved? Today?"

"Yeah. Well, I guess she's been moving stuff out for a week or so. She wanted to be done before..." He tilts his head and snaps his fingers a few times. "Wait a minute! You're the guy! The one she's obsessed with!"

This is a turn of events I wasn't expecting.

I hold my hand out. "Mike Kesso."

He takes it, his handshake firm. "Harrison Danvers."

"Now, when you say obsessed..." I arch a brow.

Harrison leans against his doorframe. "I mean, she had a photo of you next to her bed and blushed her face off when I asked her about it." He must see my expression change because he waves me off. "It wasn't like that. I just offered to help her carry some of her boxes out the other day, and I saw it. Well, saw *you*." He snorts.

"So you and her?" I can't stop myself from asking.

He smirks. "I don't think I'm her type."

ALICE

"Thank you." I smile, taking the steaming mug of peppermint tea from Sam.

"You're welcome."

Suzy puts an arm around my shoulder in a side hug, careful not to jostle my tea. "Go get your rest." She smacks a kiss on my cheek. "Tomorrow you're telling us *everything*."

"Yeah, yeah," I sigh. "I owe you guys."

Sam flicks at one of the buttons on my pajama shirt. "You don't owe us shit."

I run my free hand down my front, smoothing out the tiny present-shaped button. "Okay, fine. I'll live in your basement forever and never thank you again."

"That's more like it!" Suzy laughs.

Shaking my head, I move out of the kitchen, past the little entryway, and open the door to the basement.

Suzy and Sam inherited this house from their grandfather—on the other side of their family—last summer. It's a little two-bedroom rambler in an old part of town, with a tiny yard and an unfinished basement.

Being nearly as broke as me, they've been doing the renovations themselves, little by little, but the bones are there, and I know they'll make it into something special.

My descent slows when I notice the glow at the bottom of the stairs.

There are a few small, uncovered windows lining the basement that let in light from the streetlamps outside, but that's not what this is.

When my feet hit the bare concrete floor, I have to press my lips together to stop my chin from trembling.

Strung across the exposed floor beams above me are strings of multicolored Christmas lights.

I need a second to steady myself before shouting up the stairs, "I love you!"

"We love you, too!" my cousins chorus back before I hear the floor creak as they walk away from the stairs.

The main area of the basement is piled with old furniture and stacks of boxes, but in the center is a little clear spot that I call home.

Carefully, I lower myself onto my mattress that's resting on the floor.

With my nightstand next to me, it's really not much different than my old apartment.

I left everything in my nightstand when I packed it into my car earlier today—having gone back to grab the final things after the show wrapped up. So, when I open the top drawer, a familiar shoebox greets me.

Setting my tea down, I drag the box out and set it on my lap.

I pause for a moment before opening the lid.

Now that I've met Michael, it feels a little creepy to have this. A little bit serial killer. A lot a bit stalker. But I justify my collection by telling myself there are probably lots of people out there who save Chef Mike Kesso articles.

But I bet those people haven't had his face up their skirt.

I flip the lid off.

Magazine articles, interviews, and one signed photo stare up at me.

I always thought of this as my inspiration box. A way to motivate myself to follow my dreams, just like Michael did.

I don't need an empire like he's built, but just one bakery would be nice. One thing to call my own. A way to put my stamp on this world.

But now... I bite my lip. Now I wonder if this is more of an obsession box.

I use the tip of my finger to nudge the photo into view.

I won this as a part of a gift basket from a food blogger I follow. And it's been my most prized possession ever since.

I nudge it back under an article.

"Get a grip, Alice," I mumble out loud.

What we did was... fun. But it was a moment.

A moment I'll remember for the rest of my life. But just a moment.

And moments pass.

I set the box on the mattress next to me and flop onto my back.

It's time for me to figure out what I'm going to do with my life. I feel too old to be this lost. This unsure.

Staring at the lights above, I try to imagine my perfect life. What would make me happy.

Michael.

Okay, what would make me happy but is also realistic, I correct myself.

Blinking against the feeling of loss that's trying to overwhelm me, I take another slow breath.

Habit has me patting the empty pocket of my pajama pants, wishing I'd remembered to look for my lost coin.

When they finished my interview, the director, or whoever she was, told me I was free to go. I didn't want to. I wanted to stay and find Michael. Talk to him. Maybe hug him. Tell him how much he's meant to me over the years. How he's inspired me to be a better baker and to find my happiness.

But when I craned my neck past the director to look for him, all I saw was his back as he hugged Mikayla.

The rational part of my brain told me that he always hugs the winner. It's a part of every episode—the judges hugging the victor—but the sight of it went straight through my heart. And in an emotional panic, I half ran to my room, cleared out my things, and left.

Biggest mistake of my mistake-riddled life.

I groan and rub a hand over my eyes.

A loud knock at the front door has me jolting up into a sitting position.

I don't have a clock set up, but I know it's late. Late enough that no one should be dropping by.

Creaking floorboards tell me that one, or both, of my cousins are on the way to answer when the doorbell chimes.

"Geez, we're coming!" Suzy yells a moment before I hear the front door open.

A low voice joins my cousins', but I can't make out what's being said.

Standing, I take a few steps toward the stairs.

There's the unmistakable sound of Sam squealing in excitement, followed by the front door closing.

I wonder what—

The basement door opens above me, and I open my mouth to ask what's going on when I freeze.

The figure silhouetted at the top of the stairs is not Sam. Or Suzy.

My breath catches in my lungs as the form takes the first step down, closing the door behind him.

It can't be.

Frozen in place, I stare as the glow from the Christmas lights slowly illuminates the man before me.

Black leather shoes. Dark wash jeans. And the same formfitting black shirt I'd recognize in my sleep.

"Michael?" I whisper his name.

With a final step, he stops right in front of me. The soft light highlighting the strands of silver in his hair.

His eyes are on mine, and he looks… angry.

"What are you doing here?" I'm still whispering, too stunned to do more. Too stunned to even worry about the unflattering candy cane striped pajamas that I'm wearing.

His jaw flexes. "You left."

"I…" My mouth opens and closes. "I was told we were done."

Michael shakes his head. "We're not done."

"We're not?" My voice trembles.

He takes a step toward me, closing the distance between us. "Baby Cakes, we're never gonna be done."

"Michael." I breathe his name again, only this time, there's no question.

He's here.

Michael is here… for me.

MICHAEL

The needy way she says my name is all the confirmation I need.

My arms circle Alice, pulling her into my body as I crash my mouth into hers.

My Alice.

My girl.

Sliding my hands down, I cup her sweet ass and hoist her up my body.

Alice's legs instinctually wrap around my waist. The warmth of her pussy settling over my already stiff dick.

"Never run from me," I growl between kisses. "Don't ever run away from me again."

"I won't," she whimpers.

Tightening my hold, I use my grip on her ass to drag her up and down my length. "Promise me."

"I promise." She's panting now. The heat of our need lighting us both on fire.

"Damn right, you fucking promise." My teeth catch her lower lip before licking the bite away. "You're the star on top of my tree." I kiss her again. "I'm incomplete without you."

"I'm sorry for leaving," she half sobs into my mouth. "I thought—"

"Shh." I take the few steps to her mattress and drop down so my knees are on the edge, lowering her gently onto her back. "I don't need your apologies. And I'm sorry I didn't find you sooner."

She stares up at me. "You're here."

"I'll always be here. Because I need you by my side. I need you to be where I am."

Alice nods, her hair spread across the bed. "I will. I promise I will."

Her soft promises slither down my spine, making me harder than I've ever been before.

Deepening the kiss, my tongue slides against hers.

Her hands claw at my shoulders, my back… tug at my hair.

I angle my head, wanting more, and she lets me.

She tastes just as sweet as I remember. Everything I'll ever need to sustain me. Everything I'll ever need to please me.

Her hips rock up against me, and we both groan.

"Fuck, Baby. Are you ready for me? Will you let me in?" My voice is so low I hardly recognize it.

"God, yes." Her eyes are glassy when she looks up at me. "I need you."

I press my weight into her.

"You deserve gentle. You deserve tender. But that's not what you're getting tonight." I rock my length against her. "You scared me today. When I couldn't find you—" I cut myself off and slide my mouth over to her ear. "Good girls get sweet things. Naughty girls get it rough. And you've been very naughty."

The moan that rolls out of her chest makes my balls ache.

"You like that?" I lick her neck. "You want what I'm going to give you?"

"Yes! Michael, yes!"

Sitting back on my heels, I smirk at her cute as fuck pajamas. Then I grip the fabric and rip the front open. Her pretty little buttons flying in every direction.

Alice's gasp turns into a moan when I close my mouth around one of her peaked nipples. My own rumbling satisfaction drowns out the thudding pulse in my ears.

My Alice is warm and willing and so goddamn delicious.

With my mouth occupied, I shift my weight and use one hand to tug her pants down her hips.

"Christ, woman, you're perfection," I groan when I drag my mouth away from her tits.

Leaning back, I yank her pants all the way off, and she takes the moment to shimmy out of her torn top.

Standing, I yank off my shirt as Alice's breasts heave with each inhale.

My hands are undoing my zipper when my eyes catch on the open box next to Alice.

She sees the direction of my gaze and reaches for it, but I'm quicker.

Alice lets out a strangled sound as she throws her hands over her face, covering her eyes but leaving the rest of her naked form on full display.

It takes me all of a second to figure out what this box holds. Because it holds me.

All of my best interviews. All of my favorite accomplishments. All of the causes that are closest to my heart.

A huge smile pulls across my face as I set the box down on the floor, removing my pants and boxer briefs in the process.

"Sweetness, look at me."

Alice shakes her head, her tits jiggling with the motion.

I grip my dick, giving it a firm stroke. "Open those mistletoe eyes, Alice."

Slowly, she moves her hands, and her eyes widen as she takes in the sight of me. Nude. And hard.

"Does it look like I'm upset?"

She doesn't reply, only shaking her head again.

Another stroke. "Words, Baby."

"N-no, you don't look upset."

"That's right." I keep my hand on my cock as I kneel between her spread legs. "That collection of yours makes us even."

"Even?" she asks, her eyes darting all over my body.

"Yeah, Alice. Even." I line my dick up with her entrance. "Because it means you're just as obsessed with me as I am with you."

Thrusting my hips forward, I sink myself into her heat.

ALICE

*P*leasure explodes inside me as Michael fills me with his entire length.

My lips part to release a cry, but before sound can come out, a large palm closes over my mouth just as Michael's body drops onto mine. His weight pins me to the mattress.

"We gotta be quiet, Baby." His cock throbs inside me. "Those sounds are for my ears only."

His words grate against my skin, and I clench around him.

"Fuck, Sweetness," he groans. "This pussy was fucking made for me."

I nod my agreement, his palm still preventing me from speaking.

And when he drags his cock out before slamming it back in, I'm thankful that he's still muffling my cries. Because I can't hold back.

"So slick."

His hips meet mine.

"So hot."

Another thrust bounces my body beneath his.

"So tight."

His hand slides away from my mouth to cradle the back of my head.

Michael looks into my eyes from inches away, and a physical roll of emotion sweeps through my soul. A tremendous feeling of *rightness* rests over my heart. And I know this is it. This is the man I'm going to spend my life with.

With trembling fingers, I place my hands on his face and pull him closer.

His hips slow. His eyes show understanding. Like he's feeling the same thing I am.

"My Alice." His quiet claim brushes over my lips.

"I'm yours," I reply.

His mouth claims mine. His tongue matching the motion of his thrusts. His whole being filling me.

Michael. He's mine. Truly mine.

I roll my hips to meet his. "My Michael."

A shudder rumbles through his body.

Fully seated inside me, he pumps his hips, pushing even deeper.

"Say it again." He grits the command in a harsh whisper.

My hands scratch down his neck until my palm is flat over his thumping heart. "You're my Michael. No one else's."

The hand not behind my head slides over my side, and he pulls back enough to slip it between us.

"Tell me the rest," he demands.

His fingers flex against my belly as they inch lower. And lower.

When his thumb brushes through the moisture between us, I close my eyes. And when he presses against my clit, I arch my back and moan.

Michael's other fingers tangle in my hair. "Tell me the rest."

"The rest?" I blink my eyes back open.

I can hardly think.

His thumb traces a small circle.

What was the question?

His thumb starts to rub harder as he pulls his cock out until just the head of him is still inside me.

"Tell me what you feel."

My eyes slide shut again. "I…"

He pushes back inside me.

"I…" Joy fills every one of my cells as my orgasm starts to spark beneath his touch.

"Tell me, Baby."

"I love you."

My eyes pop open in panic. I didn't mean to say that.

Except Michael's not pulling away.

He's not holding back at all.

His hips slam into mine.

"Say it again," he growls. Each thrust sliding us farther up the mattress.

"I love you." I cling to his neck, and I feel tears fill my eyes.

He presses his forehead to mine. "I love you, too. So goddamn much."

I lose the battle against the tears. The intensity of the moment is too much. Too overwhelming.

"Say it again." I choke out my own demand.

"I fucking love you, Alice Hatter." Michael's own eyes are glassy. "I'm gonna love you forever."

His thumb brushes over my clit once more, and I combust.

Sobs mix with moans of ecstasy as I pulse around him. Pulling him in as close as he can get.

"Alice," he chants into my neck. "My Alice. My Sweetness. I'm so close."

"Let go, Michael."

He starts to withdraw, but I hook my feet around the back of his thighs. "Come inside me. I want you to come inside me."

I can feel every muscle in his body tense, and I hold him tight against me as he roars his release.

MICHAEL

*C*ollapsing, I pull Alice with me as I roll to the side, not wanting to crush her.

We're a tangle of hot and sweaty limbs as we work to catch our breaths, but I still pull her into my side, not ready to lose contact.

"I'll clean you up in a minute." I kiss the top of her head. "But not yet."

Alice snuggles her cheek against my chest, making a sound of contentment.

I kiss her hair again, the twinkling lights above us casting a colorful glow on her golden locks.

I can feel her smile on my skin. "Did you say I had *mistletoe eyes?*"

"Uh-huh." I stroke my hand down her back. "They're green, like mistletoe." I palm her ass. "And I want to kiss everything below them."

She shakes her head, letting out a snort of laughter, and we settle into each other further.

Her hand splays over my stomach, and I feel her back rise, like she's inhaling to speak, only she doesn't say anything.

I close my free hand over hers. "What's going on in that beautiful brain, Baby Cakes?"

Her fingers shift until they're entwined with mine. "What does it mean?" Her shoulder lifts in a little shrug. "Are we dating now?"

A chuff escapes me, and I feel her tense against my side.

Before she can pull back, I drag her over my body until she's sprawled across me.

"Look at me." I wait until her vulnerable eyes meet mine. "I'm yours. And that wetness leaking out of you, soaking my cock, that marks you as mine. There's no one else. For either of us."

Alice blinks, and I know she can feel the truth in my words.

"So yeah, we're dating for the next few days, or however long it takes me to find you the perfect ring. And after that, you'll be my fiancée. Then, if I have my say, I'll be calling you wife by the time the clock strikes midnight on New Year's Eve."

ALICE

*P*eace like I've never felt before wells inside me, and I find myself shedding tears of happiness for the second time tonight.

"I think I can live with that." The side of my mouth pulls up in a soft smile.

One of his large hands grips my ass. "Good. Because I can't live without you."

I shake my head at the ridiculousness of it all. "People are gonna think we're being irrational. Or that we're faking it."

He pulls me higher, so my mouth is aligned with his. "Let them think what they want. We know the truth. That's all that matters."

I brush my lips over his. "There's still so much to talk about."

"We have all the time in the world." He shifts his hips, and I feel him harden beneath me. "Starting with our flight to Canada tomorrow."

"We're going to Canada?"

"Yeah."

"Tomorrow?" I ask.

"Yeah, Sweetness. Tomorrow." His lips graze against mine. "Anywhere I go, you go, too."

Proving his point, Michael seals his lips to mine, then rolls us over. Sinking back inside me.

EPILOGUE – ALICE

"Be safe." Sam's arms tighten around me while we stand on the front step in the cold.

"I will." I sniff, hugging her back.

Suzy, who just got done crushing my ribs, wipes at her eyes. "Don't start crying again! I don't want to have red eyes all freaking day!"

I smile through another sniff, stepping back from my cousins. "I love you guys so much."

"We love you too," Sam says with a watery grin as she glances behind me.

I know what she sees: a handsome-as-sin man waiting for me to climb into the back of a hired SUV with him and head to the airport.

Honestly, I think my cousins were less surprised than I was when we came up the stairs this morning and announced that I'd be leaving with Michael to go shoot a *Second Bite New Year's Special* in Canada.

Canada!

My mouth pulls into a broad smile. "I'm going to Canada."

They grin back, Suzy reaching out to shove at my shoulder. "I told you it wasn't a waste to get your passport."

"You were right," I agree.

I've always wanted to travel the world but have never had the opportunity, or means, to leave the country. It was a completely random desire that had me filling out the paperwork last summer. Wanting to be prepared, just in case an opportunity arose. And I'm glad I did.

"I'm sorry I'm missing Christmas," I whisper, causing them both to roll their eyes at me.

"Alice, if Santa gave me a gift like that for Christmas, I'd ditch you both in a freaking heartbeat," Sam states, making Suzy snort.

"You guys signing me up for *Second Bite* was truly the best present I've ever received." Looking over my shoulder, my heart softens when I lock eyes with Michael.

"You ready, Baby Cakes?" His voice is gentle, and I fall in love with him even more.

The girls snicker at the use of his nickname for me, but I still give them one more hug before I turn away and walk toward Michael. Toward my future.

EPILOGUE II – MICHAEL

"Terminal one," I tell the driver, settling back against the seat.

Snowflakes start to fall as Alice waves out the window to her family, and I'm hit with a wave of immense honor.

She's chosen me.

She's chosen to drop everything in order to spend time with me.

I unbuckle my seat belt and slide into the center of the bench seat, putting myself against her side.

Alice grins up at me. "What are you doing?"

My hand grips her thigh. "I was too far away."

Her head shakes, but her fingers close over mine. "I guess you can stay, but you need to put a seat belt back on."

One-handed, I find the center belt and click it into place. "You worried about me, Baby?"

She slides her hand over to my thigh. Her little fingers gripping the broad muscle, mimicking my grip.

"You're mine now, Michael Kesso. I'll always worry about you."

My heart squeezes in my chest.

This girl.

Alice blinks up at me with her pretty eyes, and I suddenly remember...

"I almost forgot." I shake my head at myself. Leaning back in the seat, I reach my hand into my front pocket. "I think this is yours."

Alice's smile freezes on her face when she sees the large silver coin in my palm.

"Oh, Michael!" One hand covers her mouth as the other reaches out to pick up the item. "Where did you find this?"

"In your hotel room. I went looking for you after the show wrapped up, and housekeeping was already in there cleaning. They gave it to me, assuming you'd dropped it."

Alice nods, and I hear her sniffle.

I wrap my arm around her shoulder, pulling her into my side.

"I'm okay," she whispers.

I'm worried I might have ruined our morning, but then she tips her head back and looks up at me with a smile bright enough to inspire a Christmas jingle.

Smiling back, I brush a thumb over her cheek, wiping away a stray tear.

"My grandma gave me this coin."

"The one who inspired your cream cake?" I ask, my mouth watering just thinking about it.

"Yeah, she taught me to bake." Her lips quirk. "She was pretty feisty, and I think she would've liked you."

"Damn right, grandparents have always loved me."

Alice rolls her eyes. "Sure."

I lower my forehead to hers. "We have a long flight. How about you spend that time telling me all about your grandma? I'd love to critique her recipes."

Alice playfully swats at my stomach. "You wouldn't dare."

With a sigh, she leans farther into me. "This feels like a dream."

"It's not a dream, Baby Cakes." I trace my thumb along her jawline.

Her hand closes over my wrist, holding me in place. "I've loved you for so long."

I pull her closer. "I'm jealous."

"Jealous?"

"Jealous of the extra time you got." Her grip on my wrist tightens, and I feel it in my soul. "I have so much lost time to make up for. It almost feels unfair. But I'm going to make it up to you. I may not have the words to explain to you just how much I love you. But I promise to spend the rest of my life showing you just how much you mean to me."

Alice's eyes swim with happiness as she arches up, brushing her lips across mine. "I love you, too, My Chef."

The way she calls me that has my balls tightening.

That's something to explore.

Closing the rest of the distance between us, I smile.

This is gonna be a Christmas to remember.

SNOWED IN BITE

A Tilly World Holiday Novella

S.J. TILLY

SNOWED IN BITE - PART 2

By S.J. Tilly

This book is dedicated to my friend G. Marie and her novella Snowed in Fling.
I hadn't realized I was using basically the same title as you until it was too late.
Thank you for being chill and sharing the vibes.

ALICE

I squeeze Michael's hand, and his dark eyes lower to meet mine.

He squeezes my hand back. "What is it, Baby Cakes?"

I roll my lips together and tip my head just the smallest bit to the side.

Michael's mouth pulls up on one side. "I need more than that, Sweetie."

Sweetie. Gah.

I can't believe any of this.

Literally none of it.

The last few days have been a total dream. A whirlwind. A fairytale.

But today… reality is setting in, and I don't quite know how to handle it.

I keep my voice low as I point out the obvious. "Everyone is staring."

He doesn't miss a beat. "I know. I can't keep my eyes off you either."

My cheeks heat at his insinuation that people are staring at me. But we both know that's not true. They're looking at him.

Michael is literally famous, and I'm nobody.

Well, not nobody. Not after the live-streamed episodes of *Second Bite* that played around the world three days in a row, ending yesterday.

Before that, no one had ever heard of me, but now I'm Alice Hatter, contestant from the *Second Bite* holiday special, who did fine on the first challenge, spectacularly screwed up the second challenge, got a Chef Mike Kesso Second Bite on the third challenge, and embarrassed herself more than once—stumbling over words and feet, for the world to see.

I didn't win. Not with my ice cream atrocity.

So yeah, I'm just the girl from the show.

Not the winner. Just a girl.

Now, if the world had seen the rest of the stuff that happened after the cameras turned off... like Michael coming to my hotel room and shoving his face under my skirt...

If the public knew about that, the stares would probably be wider.

Michael squeezes my fingers, and my pulse flutters through my body.

I never expected that *the Chef Mike Kesso* would end up as in love with me as I am with him.

I never could have guessed that Michael would return my years-long obsession the moment he laid eyes on me.

I never dreamed my life would change because of a television show.

But it did.

And now here we are.

Together.

In public.

And not just public but the Minneapolis International Airport, holding hands, for everyone to see.

I dart my eyes around, confirming that, yes, many people are still staring at Chef Mike, TV personality and world-renowned baker.

A man who has been famous for years. Decades honestly. And at forty-five, fifteen years my senior, he's only gotten better looking.

His masculine jawline, his salt-and-pepper features, his tattoos, his bad-boy attitude, his strong, skilled hands...

My cheeks start to heat for a whole other reason as I think of him naked, grunting and gripping me to him while his weight drives me into my mattress.

"What are you thinking of now?" His deep voice rumbles over me.

I blink up at him. "Nothing."

His grip on my hand shifts so our fingers are entwined. "You're a terrible liar."

I huff. "Don't change the subject."

"And what exactly was the subject?"

"You know." I widen my eyes. "The staring."

"Ah, yes. That."

"What do we do about it?" I ask.

Michael's smile is soft. "Nothing."

"But—"

"You'll learn to ignore it," he says like that will be easy. Like having a large percentage of the population looking at us isn't a big deal. "Come on, let's grab some breakfast."

"Breakfast?" I'm hardly one to turn down food, but nerves are eating at my stomach.

Michael uses his grip on my hand to guide me toward a sign for a bakery in the main part of the terminal. "We'll have a meal on the plane, but I'm hungry now." He smirks at me. "You wore me out last night."

I bump his hip with our joined hands. "Michael," I admonish.

"What?" He feigns innocence.

Out of the corner of my eye, I see someone taking a photo.

I do my best to ignore it.

I really do.

But I'm not a huge fan of photos. And maybe that's because candid photos of me always seem to be taken from the worst possible angles. Or maybe it's because I've always felt a little too big, always felt like my body takes up too much space in an image.

Really, it's probably because of a whole slew of things—society, childhood bullies, nineties movies…

But now, next to this tall, handsome man, I'm even more aware of my flaws. And even more stressed about my appearance than usual.

"Alice." Michael's tone is concerned, and I look up to see him frowning down at me.

"I'm okay." I try to soothe him.

"You tensed up. That's not okay." He stops walking and turns to face me, putting his back to the people passing, blocking everyone but him from my view. "I won't ever let anyone hurt you." He doesn't let go of my hand but lifts his free one to grip my shoulder reassuringly. "And my fans aren't like that, they won't do anything to you. But they will want to take photos. And, for the record, I want them to." He leans in a little closer. "So tell me the truth, Baby. What's wrong."

Take photos.

"You want them to take photos?"

He nods. "Of us together, yes. Now tell me what's wrong."

"I…" I don't know how to word this in a way that won't sound like I'm just fishing for compliments. "I just don't want to cause you problems," I say quietly.

He moves even closer. "How could you possibly cause me problems?"

I shrug, trying to brush it off, but I know I need to say it. "I don't want to ruin… your image." I gesture at him. "You're you. All handsome and fancy, and I'm…" I huff out a breath as my shoulders slump a bit. "I don't look like your exes." I swallow down the words that want to jump out, and gesture down my body at the gray scoop-neck dress my cousin gifted me because she didn't wear it much. "I'm wearing a secondhand dress."

I hate to bring up his exes, but I've seen them. He's a celebrity; everyone's seen them.

Michael has never been portrayed as a player, but he wasn't a virgin when he crawled over me last night. And the women he's been photographed with haven't been plus-size girlies. They've been... *not* plus-size girlies.

His chest expands as he takes a deep breath, and I brace myself for his reply.

But instead of speaking, he walks forward. Into me. Forcing me backward.

My mouth opens, but Michael shakes his head. "Not another word out of that pretty little mouth."

My jaw snaps shut.

After a few steps, Michael grips my shoulders and turns me around.

I don't try to defy him, keeping the pace he's set. But then I see that he's walking us toward the bathrooms.

Correction, he's walking us toward the single door for the private family bathroom, between the men's and women's restrooms.

A green light is illuminated next to the handle, letting us know it's empty.

"Michael," I hiss, trying to slow.

But he keeps a palm on my back, pushing me forward.

His large hand reaches past me and opens the door, then he applies more pressure on my back, urging me inside.

Since trying to resist him will cause more of a scene, I step into the small room.

Michael's oversized presence pushes in behind me, and I

swear I hear some snickers and gasps before the door clicks shut.

I spin around, my mind flashing to all the dirty things that could happen behind a locked door. "Michael, we cannot have sex in an airport!"

Michael's angry expression doesn't go anywhere. "We could, Sweet Cheeks, but that's not the reason I brought you in here."

"Then why—"

He takes a step closer. "I need to say a few things to you, and as much as I appreciate my fans, I don't need any of them recording this."

I clutch my hands in front of my stomach. "Then you should probably keep your voice down."

He nods once and steps farther into my space, lowering his voice. "Listen closely, then." He reaches out with one big palm and cups my chin, keeping my eyes on him. "My past *relationships* mean nothing. Not a single woman I've ever dated or been with compares to you. You are my everything. My fucking world. My future. And you are fucking stunning."

I swallow, and he rubs his thumb under my chin, feeling the movement.

I watch his own throat work on a swallow. "I don't want to tell you anything about the women I've... been with because as far as I'm concerned, they have been erased from my memory. And if I could delete all records of them from the internet, I'd do it. But if you need to hear me say it, I'll tell you the truth that the media didn't always cover. I like women of all sizes." He shakes his head. "I *liked* women of all sizes. Now..." He drags his eyes down my form. "Now I only like one size. Alice size. And if you need me to remind you just how fucking much I lust after your body, I'd be happy to demonstrate. Right now. And prove that we indeed can have sex in an airport."

Since the moment we met in person, Michael has done nothing but prove his loyalty to me. And even though I shouldn't need the reassurance, his words are everything I needed to hear. And with a sigh, I let the safety they bring wrap around me like the sparkly, happy garland on a tree.

A smile tugs at my mouth, and I reach up, placing my hands on his chest. "Have I told you how much I love you today?"

His intense gaze shifts from protection to affection. "Not yet."

I take a deep inhale, letting his scent fill my lungs. "I love you, Chef Michael."

MICHAEL

I slide my palm around to the back of Alice's neck, feeling her soft blonde curls against the back of my hand.

"I love you too, Little Miss Christmas."

As I'd hoped, her mouth pulls up into a full smile at the nickname.

She really is my Christmas miracle. My ultimate gift. And the thought of her thinking poorly of herself, in any way, lights up every cell in my body with rage.

Alice is everything I've been looking for.

Everything I've been wishing for.

She's my salvation from loneliness.

My missing ingredient.

My better half.

And with her soft gray dress, her sparkly red earrings, and her green slip-on shoes, she couldn't look more perfect.

But if she's self-conscious about her clothing, I'll buy her an entire new wardrobe. Two, if necessary.

"Give me a kiss," I demand even as I lean down and press my lips to hers.

Alice sighs, and her peppermint breath dances across my senses until all I can focus on is the warm feeling of her mouth on mine.

Her fingers dig into my chest, clinging to my shirt.

I'm tempted to rip the buttons off and peel the fabric from my body so I can feel her hands directly on my skin. But then I remember we're in a public bathroom, and a sexy scandal isn't exactly the way I want to introduce Alice to living a life of fame. I'm hoping for something more subtle, like us walking through an airport hand in hand.

I reluctantly pull back as my dick starts to throb. "Tell me you love me again."

Alice huffs out a laugh. "I love you, you bossy boy."

I reach down to adjust myself. "Good. Now let's go get something sweet to eat."

She glances down at my hand, still on my junk, before darting her gaze right back up.

Her cheeks turn pink, but I love that she hears *something sweet to eat* and looks at my dick.

I have to adjust myself again.

My fingers tighten around my length, and I groan. "Damnit, Vixen."

"What?" She snickers.

"Should've started my morning between your legs. This flight is going to kill me."

Alice smooths my shirt with her palms. "It's just a few hours, right?"

I nod.

"And then we have a couple days for your prep time?"

I nod again, confirming that production will need some time for setup.

"Well then." She taps her fingers against my chest. "It sounds like you'll have ample time to..." The pink on her cheeks deepens. *"Get between my legs."*

With my hand still on my dick, I can feel the twitch it gives at her words.

"Baby Cakes, you're killing me." I lower my forehead to hers. "I came in here to set you straight, and you're gonna have me leaving with tented pants."

Alice slides her hands around to my sides, holding on to me. "Girls are lucky in that sense."

"In what sense?"

She shrugs. "You can't see how turned on I am."

The groan that rolls out of my chest is immediate. She practically admitted that she's wet for me right now. "Fucking hell, Alice. You're not helping."

I give up on my dick and wrap my arms around her shoulders, hugging her to me.

Her body relaxes against mine before she whispers, "I still can't believe this is real."

I tighten my hug. "I can't believe you're real either."

We breathe each other in, but the moment is interrupted by Alice's stomach growling.

And the sound is enough to finally get my blood flow under control.

My girl is hungry.

So I must feed her.

"Food. Then plane. Then the hotel bed until tomorrow morning," I say, stepping back and reaching for the door handle.

"Um…"

I look back at Alice's hesitation. "What's wrong?"

She glances around the room. "I think we should wash our hands."

I can't stop my smirk. "You literally only touched me."

Alice rolls her eyes. "I know, but we're in a bathroom." She scrunches her cute nose. "I can't leave a bathroom without washing my hands."

"You're fucking adorable."

She shakes her head and turns toward the sink. But the movement means I can see her grinning in the mirror.

I step up beside her and fill my palm with soap. "Who knew my dirty girl was such a clean freak."

ALICE

ichael gives me a reassuring nod before he grips my hand, then pulls the door open.

I try to brace myself, sure that at least a few people would have waited, probably listening outside the door to see if they could hear anything untoward. But when we step into the main hallway, I realize I wasn't braced enough.

Over a dozen people are standing there, just a few feet away, and as before, they're staring.

Only this time, they're staring at me too.

Some of the women are grinning at me, and some look to be sizing me up, but all of them keep glancing at the man at my side.

We take another step together, allowing the door to shut behind us, then he lets go of my hand.

For one horrible half second, I think he's going to step away from me.

But he doesn't.

Of course he doesn't.

Michael moves closer until my side is pressed into his and

drapes his arm over my shoulders. "Sorry, I needed to have a quick word with my woman."

My woman.

The murmurs are instant, but I can't make out any individual words because my ears are too full of fluffy snow. Because, just like that, Michael has publicly claimed me.

He said he would.

I believed he would.

But still, to hear him say it, in front of a bunch of lookie-loos, half of whom have their phones raised—probably recording—feels like a pivotal moment in my life.

"Is that Alice?" someone nearly shouts, and I startle at the volume.

Then I startle at the question.

I was just recognized.

The hand draped over my shoulder grips me possessively. "Yes, this is my Alice. And if you'll excuse us, we need to secure some breakfast before our flight."

I almost expect the crowd to complain or for someone to try and stop us, but no one does. A few lift their phones higher, but most people step back.

I do my best to take subtle inhales, working to calm my nerves, then I let Michael lead me away from the bathroom.

MICHAEL

I keep a hold of Alice as I guide her toward the bakery I spotted when I flew into Minneapolis a few days ago.

A few days ago.

How quickly life can change.

Still walking, I lean over and press a kiss to the top of Alice's head.

I need to remember that she's new to this life of fame.

And that I dragged her into it, without giving her an option, so I need to make it worth it.

I need Alice to understand how precious she is to me.

Every day.

Alice leans into me, and I feel her slide her fingers into my pants pocket, her own way of holding me close.

I kiss her hair again.

Alice tips her face back. "What's that for?"

"I don't need a reason," I reply, and she rolls her lips together, trying to smother a smile.

ALICE

This man I've fantasized about for years is even better than all my dreams, and I'm not sure how to handle it.

It's like I'm living out my own festive version of Cinderella.

I bite back the urge to grin like a complete fool as we step into line at a place called Firm Buns Bakery, and I try not to snicker at the name.

The line shuffles forward, and I rest my head against Michael's body as I read the menu board mounted behind the registers.

"Know what you'd like?" Michael's voice rumbles through his chest against my shoulder.

Reluctantly, I stand up straighter so he can hear me above the general noise of the airport.

"I'm debating between sweet and savory."

"Which ones?" His gaze moves to the menu.

"The ham and cheese hand pie, or the cranberry and cream cheese Danish." My mouth practically waters as I say it.

"And to drink?"

"I can just have water." My eyes roam to the prices. "Or I can just stop at the drinking fountain."

Michael's chest rises with what can only be a sigh. "Baby Cakes, I appreciate your desire to be frugal, but I'm going to need you to tell me what you want to drink."

I let out my own sigh. "Fine, Mr. Kesso. If you want to spend a million dollars on breakfast, I'll have a peppermint mocha."

He nods. "Okay, then." And he's kind enough not to point out that the flavors I've named will clash.

"Order for Mikayla," someone farther down the bakery counter calls out, and my head automatically jerks in that direction.

A girl in her late teens rushes forward to take the white paper bag.

I relax.

It's not *the* Mikayla who just won the holiday *Second Bite*.

There was nothing wrong with her. She wasn't mean to me. But she was trying to flirt with Michael during the whole weekend, which was annoying. Though Michael did nothing to encourage her.

Then, the unwelcome image of Michael hugging Mikayla after she won flashes into my brain.

I turn my body toward Michael and glare up at him.

He keeps his arm on my shoulder, turning me into him even more.

"What's that Scrooge look for?" There's humor in his voice.

"I don't like you hugging other women." I keep my volume low, just for him.

Michael's brows raise, clearly not expecting me to say that. "I don't—"

"Mikayla," I whisper.

The corner of his mouth twitches. "That was for work, Baby. I didn't enjoy it."

"You better not have enjoyed it," I grumble.

His mouth tips up into even more of a smile. "It's just for work," he repeats.

"Fine." I straighten my stance as best I can. "But every time I see you hug another woman, I'm... I'm going to hug another man."

The smile drops off his face. "And who exactly would you hug?"

My mind races to think of an answer that will annoy him the most. "Joey," I blurt out, referencing the good-looking host of *Second Bite*.

Michael narrows his eyes and slides his hand from my shoulder to the back of my neck, holding me in place as he leans down so we're eye to eye. "It's Christmas Eve, Alice. Don't get on the naughty list now."

My pulse gallops through my veins.

His palm is so warm and large.

His presence even more so.

And every inch of my body is lighting up with the possibility of what my big chef would do to punish me.

His gaze drops to my mouth.

I catch my breath, forgetting all about the people around us. "Would you put coal in my stocking?"

Michael's exhale is rough. "I'll shove something in—"

"Next!" the cashier calls out, cutting off whatever Michael was about to say.

For the best, I'm sure.

My legs are a little shaky as we turn and step up to the counter.

The girl at the register is looking down as she says, "Welcome to Firm Buns, what can I get for..." She trails off, her mouth hanging open as she looks at Michael. "Chef... You're Chef M—"

I swear her face pales, and her hands start to shake.

"Morning." Michael nods to her.

"I-I..."

The poor girl can't seem to compose herself.

Then she looks at me.

I smile, trying to reassure her with friendliness.

The girl yelps.

Actually yelps, like she just got bit by a reindeer.

"Um, hello," I say awkwardly.

"Alice?" Her voice is higher pitched than it was before.

I lift my hand in a gesture that's supposed to be a wave, not sure how to act after getting recognized for the second time this morning.

I watch, stunned as her eyes fill with tears. "I love you."

My lips part. Then close.

Did this girl just say she loves me? Because of my three episodes on the show?

I answer the only way I can. "I love you too."

She sways.

Michael clears his throat next to me, and I glance up to see him trying not to smile.

How is he always so hot?

I turn my attention back to the girl and read her name off her apron. "Charise, would you like to sit down?"

She nods, then shakes her head. "No, no, I'm okay." Charise brushes a tear off her cheek. "You're so pretty."

A small laugh pops out of my chest at the unexpected compliment. "Thank you. You're pretty too."

Her face contorts, and she swipes at another tear. "You're just as nice as you seemed on the show." Charise's voice cracks. "And now you're..." She darts a look up at Michael. "You two were so cute on the show."

Feeling like it's the right thing to do, I reach across the counter and place my hand on her arm. "Thank you."

She sniffles, and one of her coworkers shouts out another completed order.

"Sorry. I've never met a famous person before." Charise lets out a strained laugh. "Never thought I'd be such a crier." She looks back up at Michael. "You're really great too, Chef Mike."

Michael grins. "Don't worry, I know she's my better half."

Charise sways again, and I start to really worry for her health.

"Is everything okay?" Another Firm Buns employee steps up beside Charise.

Charise waves her away. "I got it." Heaving out a breath, she nods once. "What can I get for you?"

I smile at her composure, but Michael answers before I can.

"One of your cranberry Danishes, two ham and cheese hand pies, a chocolate croissant, a peppermint mocha, a black coffee, and two bottles of water." He tips his head down to me. "Anything else?"

I resist rolling my eyes as I shake my head. "That should be enough."

MICHAEL

*A*lice's hand trembles in mine.

"Baby Cakes," I say quietly as we walk together down the Jetway.

She jumps a little, making me frown.

The expression twists something inside me. "Are you okay?"

Her yes comes out high pitched and quick.

She's not okay.

Is she having doubts?

Am I moving this too fast?

I slow our steps and swallow. "If I'm rushing you—"

"Don't be ridiculous," Alice snaps, like she's mad I'd even think such a thing.

It's the exact reaction I need.

"Glad to hear that." I squeeze her fingers.

She huffs like she's still annoyed but continues on toward the plane.

Something is clearly still bothering her or making her nervous, but I can press her when we're in our seats.

It only takes a few seconds to catch up to the people in front of us. And together we stop just a few feet from the end of the Jetway, the interior of the plane in sight.

The line moves forward.

We step forward.

And just as I open my mouth to tell Alice to go on first, she halts.

She turns and looks up at me with wide eyes. "I've never done this before. I don't know what to do."

"Never done what before?"

Alice glances at the attendant waiting for us to board. "I've never flown."

My eyebrows rise in surprise, then I lower them in anger at myself for having assumed that flying was a normal experience.

"I'm okay." She hurries on to say. "I want to go. I just don't know…"

Softness for this woman fills my chest. "Do you want me to go first?"

She nods.

I move our joined hands behind my back. "Hold onto my belt."

Her fingers slip from mine, but then I feel them curling around the belt at my lower back.

I duck my head as we step onto the plane.

"Welcome aboard, Mr. Kesso." The attendant greets me with a wide smile.

I reply with a nod and turn down the aisle.

Alice squeaks out a hello to the attendant but keeps her hold on me.

I take two steps, then stop.

"This is us," I tell Alice over my shoulder.

Her hand drops away from my belt. "The first row?"

I turn enough so I can place my hand on her back and guide her in. "You take the window."

"You sure?"

"I'm sure, Sweetness."

She rolls her lips but doesn't argue and shuffles into the window seat.

Following, I lower into the seat beside hers.

This way she can look at the view and I can keep anyone from getting too close.

ALICE

I flatten my palms on my thighs in an effort to keep them from twisting in my skirt.

I wish I had my good-luck silver dollar in my pocket, but it's in my purse, which is wedged into the pocket on the wall in front of me. It's the one my grandma gave me, and the same one I lost in the hotel room a couple nights ago when Michael had his head up my skirt. Thankfully, Michael found it and returned it to my care just this morning. But since I was paranoid about losing it again, I decided to tuck it into my purse. However, now that we're minutes away from rocketing through the air, I'm tempted to retrieve it so I can have as much luck as possible.

Michael settles his hand over mine. "There's nothing to be nervous about."

I plaster on a smile as I turn to face him. "I'm okay."

His returning smile is soft. "You're still a bad liar."

A stressed chuckle pops out of my mouth. "And you're not supposed to point out my flaws."

Michael curls his fingers around mine. "It's hardly a flaw."

He lifts our joined hands and presses his lips to my wrist.

My pulse spikes, but this time it has nothing to do with the plane.

A throat clears, and I lift my eyes to find the attendant grinning down at us. "Can I get you two something to drink before we take off?"

Before we take off? That's a thing?

I glance at the mini water bottles that were left on the armrest between Michael and myself.

I want to ask if these are for us and if they're free, but I also don't want to sound like a bumpkin that doesn't belong in first class, let alone on a plane.

"Maybe some ginger ale?" Michael suggests, and my love for him grows even more.

"Ginger ale would be nice."

After the attendant steps away, I squeeze Michael's hand. "Thank you for that."

He dips his chin. "You can thank me by never talking about touching Joey ever again."

I stare at Michael for a moment. "What?"

He leans in closer. "You're little threat earlier, about hugging Joey." He lifts a brow like he's daring me to argue. "You're not to go near him."

I lift my brow in response. "Are you going to stop hugging the winners?"

He stares at me a beat before he nods. "You'll be the only person I hug from here until forever."

I know it's a ridiculous request for me to make. I know it's for his job. But I still nod. "It's a deal."

MICHAEL

$\mathcal{A}$s the plane starts to pull away from the terminal, Alice tenses beside me.

She's holding my hand in both of hers on her lap, squeezing my fingers like I might disappear.

I need to distract her.

"So." I stretch my legs out. "When did you first become obsessed with me?"

Her quiet gasp is adorable.

I flex my fingers on her thigh. "I saw that box, remember?"

Slowly, I turn my head toward her.

Her cheeks are turning the cutest shade of pink.

"I should've made you pack it," I say, thinking out loud.

The second I laid eyes on Alice, I knew I had to have her. So discovering her little box, the one filled with news clippings and photographs of me, was a huge relief.

I'd been worried my instant need would scare her away, but if she was already obsessing over me, then it's just proof we're meant to be.

"I'm not obsessed with you." She huffs. "I'm in love with you. There's a difference."

I snort. "Not between us, Sugar Cookie. Our love is obsession, and that's okay."

She finally looks up at me. "I think I kinda like that."

I feel the plane shift direction, but Alice doesn't seem to notice. "So what was it? What did I do to catch your attention?" The way she squirms makes me smirk. "If just thinking about it makes you react like that, then you have to tell me."

Alice blows out a breath. "It was season one, episode three."

I'm sure my grin looks as wide as a nutcracker's, but I can't help it.

Alice sees my expression and rolls her eyes.

"And what in particular caught your attention that episode?" I remember all the contestants I've met, but I can't always keep track of what happened when.

Alice heaves out a breath. "You were eating a frosted donut and got some of the buttercream on the side of your mouth."

And just like that, I know exactly what she's talking about.

The innocent moment when I used my thumb to swipe the frosting off the side of my mouth and then licked it off has been spread around the internet in GIF and meme form. It was a good lesson, and I've learned to use napkins.

"I already thought you were handsome." Alice carries on. "But that moment... did something to me."

The tone of her voice is doing something to me too. And for the first time ever, I'm glad I did what I did.

She traces her fingertip across the back of my hand. "I tried not to be a freak about it, but the more I watched the show, the more I couldn't stop thinking about you. And then—"

The plane picks up speed.

"And then what?" I prompt.

Alice grips my hand but keeps her focus on me. "Then I read an article about a visit you made to a high school." Her eyes are shining now. "All those scholarships you gave out... That was really great of you."

"It was nothing."

She shakes her head. "No, Chef Michael, it was everything."

Then, with her focus on me, the nose of the plane tilts up, and we take off.

ALICE

y body jostles, and my eyes drift open.

It takes me a second to remember that I'm on an airplane and that apparently I slept through my first flight.

I blink at the gray light coming in through the window next to me. I know Canada has a lot of wilderness, but this seems like a lot.

I lean closer to the window.

I don't actually know what the Vancouver airport looks like. But I've seen enough Canadian home renovation shows to know it's a metropolis. And this...

I look out the window at the handful of single-story airplane hangars and evergreen trees as far as the eye can see.

This looks like the middle of nowhere.

"Um, Michael." I keep staring outside.

"I didn't want to wake you up and alarm you."

"Alarm me?" I turn away from the window to look at Michael.

"We—"

The overhead speakers crackle to life. "Thanks for bearing

with us through this diversion. We've landed safely in Bear Cove and have been told a few hotels in the vicinity should be able to house everyone for the next couple of nights. When the flight attendants give you the all clear to unbuckle and deboard the plane, please follow the signs to baggage claim, and airport staff will be ready to help you with your bookings. Welcome to Canada, and happy Christmas Eve."

The pilot's words bounce around in my half-asleep head as I try to make sense of it all.

"Why were we diverted?" I whisper.

"Blizzard," Michael answers.

I look back out the window.

There is no precipitation falling, but the sky is a solid gray. A sure sign of snow.

"A couple of nights?" I repeat what the pilot said.

As a Minnesotan, I'm used to big snowstorms. But I've never been stuck away from home during one.

Michael pulls his phone out of his pocket and checks the screen. "According to the radar, we have about an hour before the snow will start. And my manager just got back to me. He has a place for us."

ALICE

I can't stop myself from leaning forward as Michael drives up the tree-lined driveway.

From Michael's tone when he was on the phone with his manager earlier, I got the impression he doesn't care for the man much. But right now, the adorable Christmas cottage in front of me is nearly enough to have me breaking our new *no hugging others* rule.

"Hoppin' holidays, this place is perfect."

Michael makes a sound in his throat. "Better than crammed into one of those motels with everyone else."

"Also true, but seriously, what is this place?"

Michael pulls the Jeep—that was somehow waiting for us at the little airport—to a stop in front of the cottage.

It's one story, with a literal picket fence sticking out of the snow covering the front yard. The entire roofline is trimmed with multicolored Christmas lights, and a lit tree is visible through the large picture window.

"Some rental my manager tracked down." Michael turns off the engine. "Apparently people were supposed to be checking in tonight to spend the holiday here, but their flight never left the ground, so we were able to take over their reservation."

"It's so pretty." I feel my eyes turn into little hearts as big, fluffy snowflakes start to fall from the sky.

Before we left the airport, Michael wisely made me dig my winter jacket out of my luggage. And as I follow Michael out of the vehicle, I zip it up to brace against the cold.

Meeting Michael at the back of the Jeep, I reach for my suitcase, but he gently pushes my hand down and pulls it out himself.

Only after I insist does Michael let me help with the bags of groceries.

Across the street from the airport was the local Bear Cove mini-mart. Michael offered to let me stay in the car, but with a sign that read *We've Got Jerky from Elk to Turkey*, I had to go in and experience it for myself.

The selection was surprisingly good, and I'm sure we purchased too much, but considering we're about to spend Christmas holed up inside, it's probably better to be safe than sorry.

MICHAEL

I can't keep my eyes off Alice as we step inside the cottage.

She points at everything—the tree, the garland-trimmed window, the red and green blankets and pillows decoratively strewn across the living room furniture.

I set the suitcases down at the end of the little hallway that must lead to the bedroom and take the grocery bags from her.

Alice lets out a sound of excitement when we step into the kitchen.

The house itself is small, just one bedroom and bathroom, but the living room on the front side of the house is spacious and the kitchen overlooking the backyard is just as large.

There's a marble-topped island with stools on the far side and a little breakfast nook in front of the windows.

"Oh, look!" Alice rushes to the patio doors, lifting her hands like she's going to place them on the glass but lowering them before they make contact. "There's a hot tub."

I place the bags on the island and move to stand next to her. "Good thing it's on the back of the house."

She tips her head back. "Why?"

I settle my hand on her perfect ass. "Because we didn't pack swimsuits."

ALICE

$\mathcal{I}$ pause when I step barefoot into the surprisingly modern bathroom.

Are these floors heated?

I wiggle my toes.

Good lord, the floors are heated.

Sighing, I pull open the glass door leading into the large walk-in shower and reach in to start the water.

I've heard people talk about how they feel kind of gross after flying, and now that I've finally done it, I get what they mean.

When I mentioned wanting to wash my face, Michael told me to just take a shower and put on my pajamas while he put away the food and made us a snack.

It's hardly late enough to go to bed, but it's not like we're going anywhere, so why not start my slumber party with Michael now?

With my discarded dress on the floor and my pajamas on the counter, I test the warmth of the water, then step into the spray.

Standing under the lush stream, I close my eyes and take the moment to appreciate how much my life has changed in a matter of days.

This time last week, I was newly unemployed and moving out of my little apartment and into my cousins' unfinished basement.

I was still content with my life. And at that point, the knowledge that I was going to be a contestant on *Second Bite*—that I'd meet Chef Mike Kesso in person—that bit of joy would have been enough to get me through another thirty years.

But then our eyes met. And his attention was electric. And the pull I felt for him went from fantasy to reality.

I take a small step back, tipping my head away so the stream can hit my breasts.

When Michael came to my hotel room and our lips met for the first time, I finally knew what lust was.

Finally understood.

My pulse starts to speed at the memory.

And then my memory takes me to last night, when Michael walked down those stairs into my makeshift bedroom... that lust turned into an inferno.

I set my palms on my sides, wondering if it's wrong to touch myself thinking about Michael when he's just down the hall.

My hands slide a bit higher.

I shouldn't.

Before I can drop them, large hands clamp over mine.

"Do it, Sweetie." Michael's voice vibrates through my body and straight to the juncture between my legs. "Squeeze those big tits for me. Show me how you like it."

His large naked body presses into my back, and I feel his hard cock hot and solid against the top of my ass.

Doing as he says, I slide my hands up until they're cupping my breasts.

I've never showered with a man before. Never stood naked under this much light with a man before. But I won't let self-consciousness ruin this for me. Not with the way his body is reacting to mine.

I squeeze my breasts together, pushing them up, causing the water to cascade down my cleavage.

Michael groans and stretches his fingers past mine to pluck at my nipples.

The sensation has me arching my back, pushing my ass against his dick.

"Michael," I breathe.

He applies more pressure to my nipples. "You like that, Baby?"

I nod.

"How much do you like it?" Michael rolls my nipples between his fingers.

"So much," I pant.

"Enough to get that sugar-sweet pussy wet for me?"

It's my turn to groan, his dirty mouth doing just as much to me as his fingers.

He pinches my nipples harder. "Answer me, Alice." He rocks his hips into me. "Or do I need to check for myself?"

"I... What?" The stimulation is too much, and I can't focus on the questions he's asking me.

Michael chuckles next to my ear. "My perfect little Christmas angel, so lit up she can't even think straight."

One of his hands drops away, and I lower one of mine to catch it.

I want more.

I need more.

But when I catch his wrist, it doesn't stop him.

Michael flattens his hand on my belly but doesn't pause as he slides it lower.

"So soft." Past my belly button. "So beautiful." Down the rounded part below. "So feminine." Into the blonde curls, right above the place I want his touch most.

"Please." I dig my fingers into his wrist, wanting to feel the muscles beneath his skin shift as he touches me.

"Please, what?"

His touch is nearly there.

"Please, I need you."

Lips close around my earlobe at the same time his hand shifts and his fingers slip into me.

MICHAEL

*H*er wet heat practically pulls me in.

I clamp my teeth onto the bottom of Alice's ear, causing her to tremble.

"Holy..." Alice lets go of my wrist and slaps her hands against the shower wall in front of her.

My chuckle is strained because as much as I love seeing her fall apart, I'm right there with her.

I release her nipple and hook my arm around her waist, steadying her as I slide my middle finger deeper into her slit.

Her slickness coats my hand even as the water streams around us.

I pump my finger inside her. "I want to spin you around and kiss you." I add a second finger. "But I also want to fuck you just like this. With my hips slamming against your ass."

She groans and wiggles against my fingers.

I press my open mouth to her shoulder and breathe her in.

"Or maybe." I slide my fingers out, adding a third, teasing her entrance but not pushing in. "Maybe I should let you control how deep I go."

Keeping the tips of my fingers stretching her core, I use my other arm to pull her with me as I back up.

There's a stool in the corner that was probably put there for decoration as much as function, but it looks sturdy enough for my needs.

Alice's hands fall away from the wall, and as she shuffles backward, her inner muscles tense, trying to drag me in.

The backs of my knees bump into the stool, and I lower myself until I'm sitting on the edge, knees spread.

"One more step back," I tell Alice as I move my hands so I'm gripping her hips.

She glances over her shoulder at me. "Shouldn't I turn around?"

"No, Baby Cakes." I shake my head and let go of her with one hand to grip the base of my cock. "You're gonna stay facing that way so you can sit on my dick."

I hear her breath hitch over the sound of the shower.

My dick throbs as I give it one firm stroke.

"I've never…"

"Goddamn right, you've never." I flex my fingers into the soft flesh of her hip. "Now, be a good little girl and sit on my lap. Tell me what you want most for Christmas."

"M-Michael."

I pull her down. "Oh, you'll get me, Alice. Every day of the year."

As she lowers her hips, she reaches down to grab my thighs.

I keep my grip on my dick, lining it up where it needs to go.

"That's it, Baby. Just sit down." I urge.

"I don't think I can," she whimpers.

"You can do anything." I encourage her.

I need this.

I need her to be the one to sink onto me.

I need to know, like really know, that she wants this as badly as I do.

Alice lowers another inch, and the tip of my cock bumps into her slit.

She's so slippery, so wet and warm, I let out a moan.

"Oh, oh god." Alice grips my thighs harder.

"That's it." I let go of my dick, my tip lodged in her pussy, and raise my hand back to her hip. "Just take what you want. You're in control."

Her inner muscles flex around me, and I hiss.

"Michael." She turns her head to look back at me. "I want it all."

I open my mouth to reply, but then Alice drops her hips down until she's settled against my lap, sinking my whole length inside her.

ALICE

*M*y head falls forward, and I fight to breathe.

Michael's cock is so big it's almost a struggle to fit him.

I took him last night, but standing like this, with my muscles clenched to stay upright, he feels different. Bigger. Snugger.

Michael's groan is so loud it echoes around the shower stall.

Pride fills me.

I'm doing this.

I'm the one causing Michael to make those sounds.

I lift my hips a few inches, arching my back as I do so I can keep a hold of Michael's legs.

I'm so slick, the motion is smooth.

"Alice." Michael doesn't loosen his grip on my hips.

I lower back down, and we both groan.

Up and down again.

I'm overstimulated.

Up and down.

Every inch of me is needy. Ready.

Up and down.

My legs start to tremble.

Up and down.

The feeling of being so full is making it hard to keep my balance.

Up and down.

"I'm not gonna last," I pant out as I wiggle all the way down again.

"Me either." Michael's voice is gruff.

I'd been referring to my legs, but hearing Michael sound so close to the edge takes me right there with him.

The fingers on my hip move, sliding around to my front. Sliding down to the spot straining for attention.

"Don't come until I do," Michael demands as he strokes my clit. "Lift those hips again." He touches where we're connected, gathering more wetness. "Just a few more times."

I do as he says, straightening my legs, flexing my muscles, lifting off him.

Up and down.

Each time is just as intense as the last.

Up and down.

Each time feels just as new.

Up and down.

His fingers start rubbing circles as his cock drags against something inside me.

My core clenches.

"Once more." His words are ragged, and I swear I can feel his dick getting thicker. "One more time, Baby."

Up.

I rise until it feels like he's almost all the way out.

My thighs shake.

My lungs struggle to take in air.

And this time when Michael brushes over my clit, I implode.

MICHAEL

*A*ll at once, Alice flies off the edge.

Her body tenses.

Her pussy pulses around my tip.

And her head flies back with a loud moan.

I wrap my arm around her, my other hand still playing with her little clit, and I move my knees closer together before I jerk her back down.

She cries out as she sits firmly onto my lap, her body spasming around my length as I bury myself to the hilt.

And that's all it takes.

My body follows hers, as it will until the end of time, and I empty myself inside her.

ALICE

I give up on my seated position, having eaten my fill, and scoot down the mattress. "That was the perfect amount."

Michael grunts, setting the serving tray on his nightstand. "If you get hungry later, you can dip into Santa's share."

I lift my head to see the four chocolate-covered pretzels, three green grapes, two broken crackers, and the one strawberry left on the plate.

"Such a bounty." I snicker and drop my head back down.

After our shower, when I regained use of my legs, we stuck with the original plan of pajamas and snacks—only the snacks were in bed.

"All the cookies and milk, I'm sure he'll enjoy the change up."

"Uh-huh, sure." I roll onto my side so I'm facing Michael. "If you want to stay up…" I let my offer linger, hoping he doesn't take me up on it.

He shakes his head and shifts so he's lying down facing me. "It's been a busy few days for both of us, so we might as well catch up on some sleep while we can."

I place my hand against his bare chest, enjoying the fact that his pajamas consist only of boxer briefs. "Thank you for bringing me on this trip."

Michael gives his head a little shake. "There's nothing to thank me for, as you didn't really have an option to say no."

I smile. "I still can't believe this is real. I've lain in bed so many nights thinking of you. Imagining what you'd be like."

It feels weird to admit that to the man himself, the one whose photo sat on my bedside table for years. But his look of smug adoration lets me know that telling him was the right thing to do.

"I can hardly believe it either, future Mrs. Kesso. But it is real. So damn real."

And then he proves his words by pressing his lips to mine.

MICHAEL

*W*hen her breath evens out, I reach behind me and turn off the light on the nightstand.

Darkness settles across the room, but we left the curtains open, allowing in the glow of the outdoor Christmas lights and the moon's reflection off the falling snow.

I watch the puffy flakes as they fall on the other side of the glass and decide this is my new favorite holiday.

Carefully, I pull Alice against my chest and wrap my arms around her.

Life gave me the most precious gift, and here, tonight, I vow to take care of her in every way I can.

ALICE

*S*weet scents pull me out of sleep, and it's the most pleasant way I've ever woken up.

I stretch out, finding Michael's side of the bed warm but empty.

Michael.

I smile as I blink my eyes open.

It's Christmas morning, quite possibly my favorite day of the year, and I get to spend it with Michael Kesso.

Then I blink my eyes again.

The sight beyond the open curtains is nothing short of breathtaking.

I sit up and turn toward the view.

The backyard is small, surrounded by towering evergreens, and every inch of it is covered in snow.

Lots of snow.

And it's still falling.

The floor quietly creaks as I cross to the window, and my smile turns into a grin when I see that not every inch is covered.

A path has been shoveled to the hot tub, proving that Michael has been busy this morning.

No swimsuits and a hot tub in the snow. Merry Christmas to me.

Not wanting to miss a moment of today, I rush through my routine in the bathroom, emerging with freshly brushed teeth and my hair up in a frizzy bun. I'm still in my pajamas, a super short sleep dress with thin straps and a low-cut front—courtesy of my cousins, who slipped it into my suitcase with a Post-it that said *wear me.*

I don't know if they had already gotten it for me as a gift or if it belonged to one of them already, but if ever there was a day to wear something provocative...

And if I get cold in this skimpy outfit, I'm sure I can convince Michael to warm me up.

Following my nose, I pad down the short hall into the kitchen. And then I stop.

Before me, in the flesh, is Michael, *in the flesh.*

Literally.

His back is to me, and I can't stop staring at his ass. His *clad only in bright red boxer briefs* ass.

It's an ass I'd write to Santa for, if it wasn't already mine.

I step closer, smug satisfaction filling every inch of me.

"Looks delicious," I say in greeting.

Michael glances at me over his shoulder, smirk already in place. "Merry Christmas." His eyes travel up and down my body. "My little snow elf."

Then he turns the rest of the way to face me, and, jingle my bells, I have to swallow.

I've never seen a hotter image in my life.

Michael has put on a green apron that covers his boxer briefs, making him look naked. In an apron. In a kitchen that smells like heaven.

"Everything okay?" His tone is knowing, even as he stares at my chest.

I step forward and dip my fingers into the open bag of flour on the counter.

"I'm sorry," I say, then I gently slap my hand on his bare shoulder.

Michael lowers his gaze to the dusty print on his skin, then looks back up at me. "You don't seem very sorry."

I grin. "I'm not. You just looked too perfect."

"And now?" He raises a brow.

I purse my lips as I consider, then I dip my fingers back in the flour. "Still too perfect."

He lets my hand connect with his other shoulder, then he snags my wrist and pulls me to him. "Naughty girl."

I'm laughing when our lips connect, but Michael quickly swallows that laughter.

Chocolate and spices swirl around us as Michael deepens the kiss.

He slides his hands around my sides to my back, holding me close.

I lean into him and drag my own hands up his back, enjoying the feel of his muscles flexing under my touch.

His lips part and I slide my tongue across his, eliciting a groan from deep in his throat.

Michael lets me taste him, for one more heartbeat, before he pulls away.

"That's enough of that, Sweetness." He takes a step back. "I promised myself I'd feed you before I fucked you again."

I cross my arms. "What a grinch."

"Go sit down." He reaches for the whisk sitting on the counter, and I jump out of the way before he can pretend to swat me with it.

After circling around the island, I pull out one of the stools and settle in to watch him work.

"What are you making?" I ask.

He turns back to the stove. "Raspberry pancakes."

"Ooo."

"With a white chocolate sauce."

"Well, stuff my stocking, that sounds amazing."

Michael chuckles.

"Is that your usual Christmas morning food?" I ask as my mouth starts watering.

Michael shakes his head. "Can't say I have a usual. Normally, I'm on the road filming for the holidays."

I drum my fingers against the counter. "Technically, you are this year too."

He turns and sets a steaming mug in front of me. "This year is different."

I lift the milky drink and inhale the rich coffee steam. "Different good, right?"

"Different perfect. Though you should hardly have to ask."

Michael turns back to the stove, hovering his hand above the large flat griddle on top of the burners, checking to see if it's ready for the batter, while I go back to staring at his ass.

He reaches for the bowl of batter to his right. "Now tell me about baking with your grandmother."

I blink.

Something about admiring someone's butt cheeks while they mention your deceased relative feels a little weird.

I clear my throat. "Um..."

"You were supposed to tell me about her on the plane." He glances back at me. "But you decided to sleep instead."

I snort. "I still can't believe I did that."

Then, after taking a sip of coffee, I tell him.

I tell Michael about my grandma. How she always had these little *silver dollar chocolate chip cookies* in her freezer. How she gave me the actual silver dollar as a token of luck—and to remind me of her. How she passed her love for baking on to me.

I tell him about Christmas Eves always spent at her house. How we'd eat until we couldn't eat anymore. How the focus was always on the feast and how presents were the last thing we cared about.

"The little candle chime thing was always my favorite part of the table setting." I sigh. "I don't know what happened to it."

Michael slides another trio of pancakes into the warm oven. "The what?"

"It's a... I don't know how to describe it." I look around and spot a notebook on one of the counters. I slide off the stool and collect it, then go back to my seat. "I'm not very good at drawing." I state the obvious as I start to sketch. "I think maybe it was made of brass, but it was shiny gold and kinda looked like a skinny carousel. It had candles circling the bottom and a trio of angels on the top part. And when you lit the candles, the heat made the angels go around in a circle, causing them to chime bells on every turn." I bite my lip as I frown at my drawing. "I'm doing a terrible job describing this."

I startle when Michael's heat presses against my back.

He reaches past me to pull the notebook to the side so he can see it. "You're a better artist than you give yourself credit for."

I sigh. "And you're being kind."

Michael kisses the top of my head. "We'll find one of these chime things before next Christmas."

Next Christmas.

The sigh I let out this time is different.

Contented.

And as Michael walks back around the island, his glutes looking like holiday hams in those boxer briefs, I wonder again how I got so damn lucky.

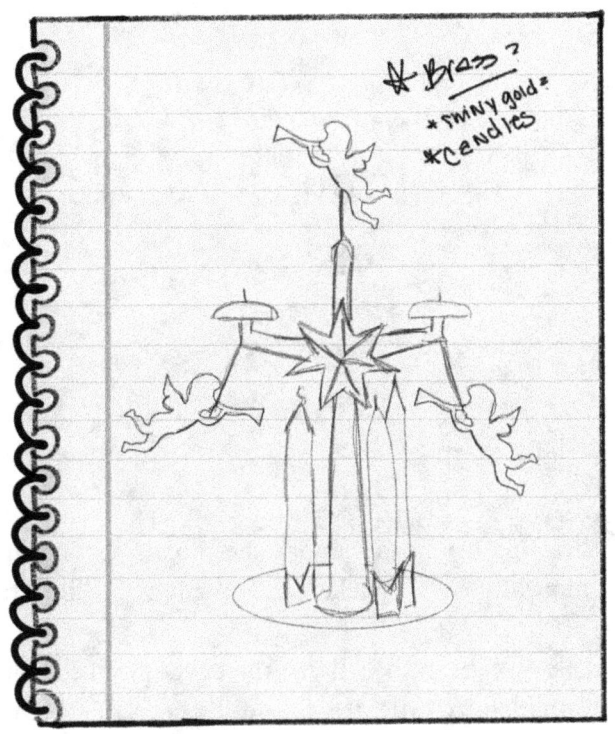

MICHAEL

*A*lice tips her head back as she moans around another mouthful of pancake, and I can't fucking take it anymore.

My dick has been half-hard since she walked into the kitchen in that slutty little dress. And it's been fully hard since she took her first bite.

"It's so good," she breathes.

And seriously, I can't wait anymore.

I never was one for delayed gratification.

Reaching behind myself, I undo the tie of my apron, then pull the fabric up over my head.

Alice finally lifts her gaze from her plate to look at me. "What are—"

I grip my cock through the thin layer of cotton as I plant my feet on the floor and push my chair back from the table. "Come here."

Her mouth drops partially open. Her eyes on my hand as I stroke myself through the fabric. And I can see the change, the hitch in her breathing, the lowering of her eyelids.

In the blink of an eye, she goes from focused on food to a horny little vixen.

"Such a responsive girl." I pull the top band of my boxer briefs down, letting just the head of my cock stick out.

"Michael," she whispers, shifting in her seat.

My eyes lower to her tits, and her nipples are straining against the fabric in a way they weren't just a moment ago. "Two seconds of watching, and your body is already priming itself for me."

Her lips move, but this time no sound comes out.

"Now come over here, Baby Cakes." I lift my hips and shove my boxer briefs down until my whole length is exposed. "And sit on Santa's dick."

Alice's fork clatters against her plate as she stands.

I lift my free hand to halt her. "Bring the sauce."

Her eyes are wide, but she doesn't argue.

Alice slides the mini carafe half-full of chocolate sauce across the table so it's next to my plate.

"Good girl." I praise her, then I pat my lap.

She takes two steps toward me, then pauses.

I narrow my eyes, but before I can question her, Alice reaches up under her skirt.

Keeping her eyes on me, she slides her panties down her legs, letting them pool around her ankles.

She steps out of them, and my heart jumps in reply.

Perfection.

Another step, and she's within reach.

I grip her hips and pull her in until she's standing next to my chair, her green eyes shining as they gaze into mine.

"Is it my turn to sit here, Mr. Santa?" Alice bats her lashes.

My dick bobs in reply.

I've never role-played before.

Never once thought of it.

But fuck me, I'm into it.

I tighten my fingers on her hips. "Climb on, Sweetie, and tell me if you've been good."

Alice reaches down and grips my cock.

My eyes start to close at her touch, but I force them back open.

I'm not missing a second of this.

"That's the thing," Alice whispers as she lifts her leg over my lap, "I don't think I've been very good." She points my dick at her entrance, balancing herself with her other hand on my shoulder.

My lungs struggle to fill. "What have you been, Little Alice?"

Her mouth pulls up on one side in a devious smile. "I've been bad. Very bad."

Then she drops down, and my cock is swallowed by her heat.

"Fuck." I half groan, half shout as her bare ass connects with my thighs, her pussy surrounding every inch of my dick.

The sneaky look that had been on her face is replaced by one of shocked ecstasy.

She impaled herself on my dick, and now she's reaping the consequences.

I dig my fingers into her sides, holding her where she is, keeping her snug on my lap, as her muscles flutter around me.

"So bad," I groan.

She nods. "So, so bad."

The morning sun is streaming in through the window behind me, illuminating her like some sort of magical winter sprite.

Her golden hair is practically glowing, and I let go of her hip and pull her hair free from the bun she'd tied it up in.

The messy curls drop around her shoulders, and I flex my hips, forcing my cock just a bit deeper.

"You know what happens to bad girls?" I growl.

Alice shakes her head, her curls bouncing with the motion.

"They have to do as they're told." I stretch my arm out and hook the handle for the sauce. "And I'm telling you to sit very still."

My voice is scratchier than normal. Rough. And I know this is going to be as torturous for me as it will be for her.

Alice grips my shoulders. "I'll try my best."

But even as she says it, her pussy contracts around me.

I click my tongue. "So naughty." Then I yank down the front of her dress.

ALICE

*M*y breasts spill free, my already hard nipples pebbling further as they're exposed to the cool air.

"So delicious," Michael says.

And then something warm is running down my chest, and I can't sit still anymore.

MICHAEL

*T*he white chocolate sauce runs down Alice's chest, trailing a line down one of her big, glorious tits.

It's graphic.

Vulgar.

And enough to send a pulse of release seeping out of my dick.

Then she starts to squirm.

Every movement she makes squeezes around my already straining cock.

Her tits bounce, and I wait until the perfect moment, wait until the sauce makes its way to where I want it before I tell her what to do next.

ALICE

"Feed it to me," Michael demands.

The creamy sauce has dripped down to my nipple, and nothing in this world could stop me from doing what Michael says.

I let go of his shoulder and grip my breast, lifting it, holding it up, so he can—

Michael flattens his tongue against my nipple and licks.

He licks and licks.

He leans closer and licks up my breast, lapping up the line of chocolate.

He moans and groans, and when he works his way back down, he sucks my nipple into his mouth.

I can't take it anymore.

I keep doing what he asked, I keep feeding him, keep my grip on my tit. But I also move my other hand down and reach under the skirt of my dress.

MICHAEL

I feel her fingers between us. Feel them moving. Rubbing at her clit.

I drag my teeth over her sensitive skin. "Such a bad girl. Touching herself without permission."

"I'm sorry," Alice cries, but she doesn't stop. "I'm sorry. I have to."

Instead of pouring the sauce, this time, I dip two fingers into the dish.

I swipe the chocolate across her other nipple.

"You have to what?" I ask, working to sound unaffected while accepting that I'm punishing myself with this more than I'm punishing her.

"I need to come." Her movements are getting more frantic. "Please, Santa. Please let me come."

My cock throbs.

"Suck my fingers clean." I lift my chocolate-smeared fingers to her mouth. "Suck them clean, and you can come, Little Alice."

I close my lips around her nipple and push my fingers into her mouth.

She sucks on them like they're made of candy, her tongue swirling around, drawing off every speck of sweetness.

She's trembling.

Moaning.

Sucking and rocking.

And then she's exploding.

Her mouth opens, and my fingers press against her tongue as she arches her back and comes all over my cock.

I can't sit still anymore.

Wrapping my arms around her, I stand.

ALICE

My world tips.

Stars are still bursting behind my eyes, and I hear something scrape across the table, then I'm on it.

My back connects with the solid wood of the breakfast table, and my legs hitch up, my heels digging into Michael's back.

I think I might be chanting something.

Maybe his name.

Maybe a prayer.

My body is still thrumming.

And then Michael starts to fuck me.

MICHAEL

I snap my hips forward, slamming my full length deep into Alice's sweet pussy.

I thrust again and again.

The plates rattle. Coffee sloshes out of the mugs onto the table. And I keep going.

I can't stop.

This is my woman.

My woman, who just climbed onto my lap.

My woman, who let me lick chocolate off her tits.

My woman, who sucked on my fingers as if they were my cock.

My woman, who just came all over my fucking lap.

And I need to claim her.

I need to mark her.

I need every inch of her to understand that she's mine.

Alice reaches for me, and I lower myself over her.

I don't stop moving.

Don't stop sliding in and out of her heat.

She wraps her arms around my neck and pulls my ear to her mouth.

"I've been so bad," she whimpers.

My balls tighten.

"Teach me a lesson and fill me full," she pleads.

I slam my hips forward one last time, then I do exactly as she said, and I fill her to the brim with my Christmas cream.

ALICE

*M*ichael hangs up his phone. "I have bad news."

I lift my head from his lap to look back at him. "What is it?"

He strokes a hand down my hair. "Our flight out is tomorrow."

I bite down on a smile. "That's bad news?"

Michael nods. "I was hoping for another week or two here."

My grin breaks through. "Maybe we can rent it out again." Then my grin falters when I remember how absolutely broke I am.

Michael pulls on my shoulder, rolling me onto my back, and glides his thumb across my lower lip. "What's that sudden frown for?"

I heave out a breath and try to sit up, but Michael places his hand on my chest, holding me in place.

"I want to help..." I wonder if there's a delicate way to talk about this.

He tips his head. "Help with what?"

I lift my hands and let them drop onto my stomach. "With renting this place. Or buying groceries. Or plane tickets..."

Michael shakes his head. "You don't have to do any of those things."

"I—" I can't say this lying down.

Twisting my fingers with Michael's, I pull his hand to the side so I can sit up.

He lets me this time, but when I turn to face him, he grabs my free hand with his so we're as entwined as possible.

"I moved into my cousins' place because the company I'd been working for... closed." I let my cheeks puff out on an exhale. "I don't even know if it was bankruptcy or what, but my last handful of paychecks bounced, and I've accepted that I'll never get that money."

"Baby—" Michael starts, but I squeeze his hands.

"I'm not telling you as some sort of sob story. I just want you to know. And I want you to know I'm not interested in your money." His lips pull up into the softest smile. "I only want you, Michael. And I don't expect you to just start paying for my life. Okay?"

He dips his chin. "Anything else?"

I shrug. "I have a little bit of credit card debt, but even with low-income scholarships, I couldn't afford to go to college, so at least I don't have student loans." When Michael starts to frown, I flex my fingers in his again. "That's a good thing. And learning from you will be better than any college class."

He sighs. "First, I'll teach you anything you want to know, but you've proven yourself to be an accomplished baker already." He closes one eye. "Just not so skilled with Jell-O."

My mouth drops open. "Too soon."

Michael's lips twitch.

I can't believe he brought that up, but it did take that hint of sadness off his features, so I guess it's okay.

"Second." He continues. "If you want to take classes, we'll make it happen." I open my mouth to retort, but it's his turn to squeeze my fingers. "Third, you're mine. And I take care of what's mine. I know you're not after my money. And I appreciate that. But you're the love of my life, Alice, and I'm going to use my considerable fortune to spoil you until the day I die. Even if you had money, I wouldn't let you spend it."

"Michael—"

"Fourth, fifth, whatever number we're on." He talks over me. "If you want to work, we'll find something for you to do. But only if you really want to."

I chew on my cheek. "Like what?"

"Anything." He thinks for a second. "Maybe something with scholarships."

A lightness fills my chest. "Really?"

Michael nods. "Yeah. I've supported a lot of causes, but I've never started one on my own. We could have our own foundation that sponsors culinary students. Do fundraisers, whatever."

My poor heart thuds inside my ribs. "You mean it, don't you? You'd really do it?"

He lifts his brows. "What? Like it's hard?"

I narrow my eyes at the older man before me. "Did you really just quote the movie I think you did?"

"No idea what you're talking about, Baby Cakes."

I keep my eyes narrowed for another moment, then use my hold on his hands to pull myself forward until my weight shifts to my knees and I can throw my arms around his neck. "Thank you, my Chef. I love you."

Warm lips press against the side of my neck. "I love you too." A beeping sounds from the kitchen. "Now give me a kiss before our dinner burns."

MICHAEL

"*A*ha!" Alice shouts in triumph from down the hall.

I finish drying the pot in my hands and set it down on the counter. "What's going on back there?"

"One sec!" Her words are followed by muttering I can't make out.

Attempting to be patient, I move my attention to opening the bottle of local Bear Cove wine I bought at the mart.

Patience is hard around Alice since I want to have my hands on her every damn second.

I know we've only been together a couple days, but I don't think this feeling is ever going to fade. This need for nearness that I have.

But I'm trying to control myself.

For instance, I sat through our entire dinner without putting my dick in her.

Bravo for me.

I pour two glasses of the deep red liquid, then bring one to my nose.

Impressed by the smell, I'm taking a sip when Alice steps into the kitchen, clutching a fluffy white robe around her body.

"They're made for skinny people." She sticks a leg forward, causing the robe to part around her upper thigh, demonstrating that the opposing sides of the robe are barely touching. "But they'll do."

I take another sip of wine. "What are you wearing under there?"

Alice bites her lip, then she quickly pulls the robe open, then shut, showing me exactly what she's wearing underneath the robe.

Which is nothing.

My blood heats, and I tip the wine glass back, swallowing the rest of it in two gulps.

Alice laughs. "What are you doing?"

"Fortifying my patience."

She wraps an arm around herself, holding the robe in place, and reaches for the second glass on the counter. "Is it working?"

I shake my head and step toward her.

She takes a step back, aiming toward the sliding glass door that leads from the kitchen to the patio. "Your robe is on the bed."

"Is that so?" I take another step.

She matches it with her retreat.

She takes another quick step toward the door. "Bring the bottle when you come out."

ALICE

*S*team dances up from the surface of the hot tub, and I sink down farther until the water is lapping at my chin.

Michael came out before dinner to make sure the temperature would be perfect, and with the glow of the moon and the twinkle of the Christmas lights… perfect it is.

The snow stopped falling this afternoon, and by evening, the roads—and our little driveway—were plowed.

I'm excited for Vancouver. Excited to travel more. To see the set for the New Year's special Michael has to record. But I'm equally excited to spend the rest of this evening with Michael—alone. Out here, surrounded by towering snow-covered evergreens.

The sound of the patio door opening has me sitting up.

Michael is gripping his robe closed with one hand, and in the other is his glass and the bottle of wine.

"Hi." I greet him shyly.

He stops at the edge of the hot tub and sets the glass and wine down on the flat rim.

"Hi, Baby." His tone is casual as he releases his grip on his robe, revealing his hard cock.

I choke on nothing. The winter air crystalizing in my lungs.

Michael shrugs out of his robe and drapes it over the deck railing next to mine.

It shouldn't come as a surprise, his nakedness. He's wearing exactly as much as I am. But, for some reason, I hadn't expected him to walk out hard.

He curls his fingers around the base of his dick. "Watch your wine, Sweetness."

"Huh?" I look up at his face, then register what he said and look down at the glass in my hand.

A few drops of wine drip over the rim of my tilted glass, disappearing into the churning water below.

"Oops." I right the glass as I return my gaze to Michael's cock.

I can't take my eyes off it.

Can't stop staring at the thick vein running the length of it.

Can't stop my mouth from watering at the sight of it.

Then it disappears under the water.

I expect him to come to me.

Expect him to cover my body with his.

But he moves to the opposite side of the hot tub from me and lowers himself onto the seat.

Silently, we watch each other.

I take a large drink of my wine, and he pours himself another glass.

When he holds out the bottle, I hold out my glass, and I let him top it off.

I've heard the warnings. How mixing booze and hot tubs can be dangerous.

I've heard them, and I've ignored them.

But now that I'm here, finishing off my extra full glass, I think I understand.

Though I'm hardly discouraged from doing this again because even though we just ate, I feel... hungry.

MICHAEL

*A*lice sets her empty glass down and slowly slides forward on her seat.

My dick hasn't gotten any softer since I got into the hot tub, and now, as she nears, it's getting impossibly harder.

Fingertips brush against my knees. "Will you do me a favor?"

Her voice is husky, and it sends a shiver down my spine. "Anything you want."

She runs her fingers up my thighs, stopping halfway. "Will you sit up on the edge?"

My stomach muscles clench. "Why?"

She drops her gaze to my lap, even though my arousal is hidden in the water.

"Because I'd like to suck your cock." She lifts her eyes back up to mine. "Please."

ALICE

*M*ichael lurches forward, capturing my face in his hands.

"You never have to say please for that, Mrs. Claus. You can put my dick in your mouth anytime you want."

Mrs. Claus shouldn't sound so hot, but after role-playing earlier, calling him Santa, the nickname hits me right in the chest.

Michael closes his mouth over mine.

We both open. Our tongues tasting the same. Like wine and lust and love.

I reach for him.

Cling to him.

He wraps his arms around me and pulls me against him.

My legs go on either side of his hips.

It's the same position we were in this morning, but the weightlessness of being in water means that I'm floating above his lap.

Michael utilizes this and moves his hand into the gap between us.

Blunt fingers slide between my folds.

Michael groans, finding me wet.

Then he pushes one of his fingers inside me, and my groan matches his.

My head swims.

Heat swirls around inside me.

And I rock my hips, fucking myself against his hand.

His lips never leave mine as he consumes my sounds.

Then something presses against my clit.

I think it's his thumb at first, then I realize it's bigger.

Much bigger.

I pull my head back and suck in a breath.

Michael has both hands between us. One with fingers buried inside me. The other gripping his cock and rubbing the head against my clit.

"Feel good?" he asks against my neck.

I moan and nod. "So, so good, Mr. Claus."

Teeth scrape against my skin. "Say that again."

"You feel so good, Mr. Claus." I dig my fingers into his shoulders, holding myself close, and I lean into the feeling of his cock against my clit.

"My Mrs." He increases the speed of his fingers moving in and out of me. "My pretty little Mrs. Claus getting herself off on the big man's lap."

His fingers twist inside me, and his cock presses into my clit just right. And my orgasm hits me like a snowball to the face.

I arch my back, my cry decorating the trees around us.

My body clenches.

My pussy squeezes his fingers.

And my heart triples in size.

"Mr. Claus," I pant. "I love you so much."

"Show me," Michael growls.

He pulls his hands free of my body and stands, stepping onto the footrest so his cock is just above the surface of the water.

His hands tangle in my hair. "Show me how much you love me."

MICHAEL

*A*lice keeps her eyes on mine as she opens her mouth wide.

And when her pink tongue peeks out, I lose my last shred of control and surge my hips forward.

ALICE

*M*ichael shoves his cock down my throat.

It's rough.

Frantic.

And perfect.

My eyes water.

I struggle to keep my throat muscles from seizing.

And I grip his thighs for balance.

"That's it." He pulls out and shoves back in. "Breathe through your nose, Baby Cakes. Just breathe and let me fucking take this throat."

I do.

I inhale and grip his legs tighter.

I blink at him.

I take in the primal look in his eyes.

And my core throbs.

"That's my girl." His cock almost slips free of my lips.

He pushes back in, his tip sliding even deeper this time.

"That's my good girl, earning her way back to the nice list."

Tears roll down my cheeks, pleasure and happiness swelling inside me.

Michael's hands flex in my hair, and the pull brings me right back to the edge.

I let go of him with one hand and reach down to that spot between my thighs.

The water has done nothing to wash away my slickness, and my fingers slip over my clit.

I moan around his length, and Michael uses his hold of my hair to pull me off his dick.

"Are you touching yourself, Little Alice?"

I nod, gasping for breath.

He drags my face forward, and I lick the slit at his tip.

Michael moans. "Rub that clit for me. I want you coming as you swallow me down."

I wrap my lips around the head of his dick, and he shoves his hips forward.

The sounds he's making...

The feeling of him filling my throat...

And my fingers on my already sensitive center...

I start to come, clamping my thighs together, trapping my hand in place even as I keep rubbing my clit.

"Fuck. That's it. Yeah, that's it, Baby. Come on those fingers." Michael jerks his hips forward.

His hands hold me still.

Holds himself deep in my throat.

"Now swallow."

It's the only warning I get.

His cock pulses in my mouth, and he starts to come.

I swallow.

I try to take it all.

But I'm not good at this.

It's too much.

I have to pull back, and his cock slips free from my mouth as I suck in a breath.

His hand is suddenly around his length, jerking it off, and the last two jets of release land across my lips and chin.

We're both panting.

Both gasping for breath.

I pull my hand out from between my thighs and grip his leg again.

"S-sorry," I heave.

Michael slowly shakes his head. "What the hell are you apologizing for?"

I reach up and run my fingers through the mess on my face. "I couldn't take it all."

Michael groans, and I watch as more release pulses from his cock. "You took fucking plenty."

I slide my fingers into my mouth, and Michael groans even louder, lowering himself into the water.

"Take anymore and you're gonna fucking kill me."

ALICE

*S*ettled in my seat, I pull my phone out of my purse to put it in airplane mode and see I have a pair of missed calls, one from each of my cousins.

The flight attendant is already walking down the aisle, so instead of calling them back, I open our group chat and send them a text, letting them know we're about to take off and that I'll call when we get to our hotel.

Michael places his hand on my thigh as he leans his head back. "You okay?"

I tuck my phone away and place my hand over his. "I'm so okay."

The side of his mouth pulls up. "Good."

I lean my own head back. "Thank you for the best Christmas ever."

His fingers flex around my thigh. "Not something you need to thank me for, Sweetness."

"All the same." I let my eyes close.

With the short drive to the airport, we didn't have to get up early. But we stayed in the hot tub longer than we probably should have and then took our time showering off afterward. Meaning we're both exhausted and I'm happy to nap my way to Vancouver.

Which is probably the smart call because I have a feeling things are going to turn up a notch when we get there.

MICHAEL

I'm used to people staring. It happens everywhere I
go. But this…

I glance around as we walk through the Vancouver airport.

This is a little more attention than I normally get.

I tighten my hold on Alice's hand.

She glances up at me with a smile. "This airport is really
nice."

I nod, agreeing, glad she doesn't seem to be stressing about
all the eyes on us.

No doubt word has gotten out that I've made Alice mine.

I knew the photos taken in the Minneapolis airport would
get around.

And I knew it would cause a buzz.

But I didn't think the good people of Canada would care this
much.

A flash goes off to my right, and I let go of Alice's hand to
drape my arm over her shoulders.

My protective instincts are flaring, and I need to settle down
before I snap at someone and make an even bigger spectacle.

I spot a little convenience shop up ahead and steer Alice toward it.

"I'm gonna grab us some waters." I bend down a little so Alice can hear me. "We need to stay hydrated after travel."

"Probably smart." She bobs her head. "And I could go for a juice, if that's okay."

I hug her to my side. "Of course it's okay. Whatever you want, Baby."

I don't drop my arm until we're standing in front of the beverage coolers, then I use both hands to grab two large water bottles. "Grab whatever else you want. We'll order up some room service when we get to the hotel, but grab a snack now if you're hungry."

Alice grabs a bottle of cranberry juice. "Maybe just something small."

She turns to the racks behind us—with the granola bars, breath mints, and magazines.

Her juice idea actually sounds pretty good, so I shift both waters into one hand so I can grab my own.

My fingers are just about to graze the plastic when Alice lets out a choked cry.

My heart leaps into my throat, and I spin around, expecting to see someone accosting my woman.

But she's alone.

Standing only a few feet away from me.

Holding up one of the tabloid magazines.

"What is it?" I step up behind her.

"It's..." She lifts the tabloid, the paper shaking in her hands. "It's us."

ALICE

$\mathcal{M}$y mouth opens, but I don't know if I want to laugh, cry, or scream.

Because...

I close my mouth and swallow down the deranged sound that's trying to burst out of my lungs.

I read the caption below the photo.

While snowed in at Bear Cove, Chef Mike gets more than a Second Bite *of contestant Alice Hatter. More photos on page eight.*

More photos.

Meaning they have more photos than the large one printed across the front page of the cheap tabloid.

I move my eyes over the photo again, taking in the look of bliss on my face as the sun shines off my loose hair. My head tipped back. My hands digging into Michael's bare shoulders. His fingers... in my mouth.

"How?" I whisper.

How is there a photo of us mid-fuck on the kitchen chair?

It's graphic.

Lewd.

But you really can't see anything that you shouldn't. Except for Michael's bare back, his body blocking the front of mine.

And you can probably guess that he's sucking my nipple into his mouth, but you can't see it.

Something warm stirs in my center.

We look hot together.

"Turn to the other photos," Michael says with his chest against my back, looking over my shoulder.

I flip to page eight.

And this time I do make a sound.

Because that's Michael's dick in my mouth.

MICHAEL

I should not be getting hard right now.
I should not *be getting hard right now.*

But looking at a photo of my hands tangled in Alice's hair, her face just above the surface of the hot tub... It doesn't matter that they've blurred out the inches of visible cock between my body and her lips, it's clear what we're doing.

Crystal fucking clear.

I ignore the words printed on the page and look at the other photos.

Another of us in the hot tub, taken before the face-fucking moment, with Alice on my lap, my mouth on her neck, and enough body contact to know we're doing more than kissing.

The last photo is back in the kitchen.

And it's my bare ass.

I groan at that one.

Not exactly the image I've been crafting for myself over the past couple decades. But the sight of Alice's little feet digging into my back, pulling me closer, still has my cock thickening.

It's all pornographic, but Alice's naughty parts are covered in every image. All of the naked bits are mine.

Which is good because I'm going to ruin the photographer when I find them. But if they'd shared more of Alice, I'd be ending their life, not just their career.

"What... I..." Alice croaks, and any stirring below my belt stops when it sounds like she might cry.

I step around her and crouch down, putting my face in front of hers.

A face that's biting down on a smile.

She slaps a hand over her mouth just as a laugh bubbles out.

"You're okay?" It's a stupid question, but I ask it anyway.

Alice lifts a shoulder. "I should probably be more horrified than I am."

"But?"

A peep of laughter slips out. "I can't help but notice how good we look."

I smirk. "They're pretty hot photos."

She nods, hand still over her mouth. "They are."

I pull Alice into a hug. "I love you, Baby. And I promise I'll take care of this."

ALICE

A large black SUV with tinted windows pulls up in front of us.

A few more people were taking pictures of us as we passed through the airport to get our luggage, but I kept my gaze down and the tabloid tucked under my arm.

Michael presses his hand against my spine, urging me into the back seat of the SUV.

I go without protest, knowing that one of the show producers is the one picking us up.

The producer, a.k.a. driver, helps Michael get our bags into the back, then they both climb in, Michael in the back next to me.

"So," the producer starts as he pulls away from the curb, "you two sure know how to make an entrance."

Michael just grunts, but my worry starts to kick in.

"Is this, um, situation, going to ruin anything for *Second Bite?*" I have to ask.

The producer laughs. "Hell no. Our projected viewership just shot through the roof."

My eyes widen. "Seriously? Why?"

"Because." The producer glances over his shoulder at me. "Pamela got sick and can't make it to the recording."

"Pamela," I whisper the name of the woman who always judges beside Michael.

The man nods. "Yep. And we just announced you as her replacement."

NEW YEAR'S BITE – PART 3

S.J. Tilly

NEW YEAR'S BITE

A Tilly World Holiday Novella

S.J. TILLY

This book is dedicated to my readers who love to bake.
I love to eat.
We're a match made in fiction.

ALICE

"*H*is dick looks huge," my cousin Suzy exclaims the second the phone connects.

Sam, sister to Suzy and my other cousin, hums her agreement.

"Hush," I hiss, looking at Michael to see if he can hear them.

But his back is currently to me as he paces through the hotel suite with his phone to his ear, so I'm pretty sure we're safe.

"Oh shit, is Mr. Huge Dick with you?" Suzy barely lowers her volume. "We're not on speaker are we?"

"Suzy." I try to scold her while keeping my volume down.

"What? It's a compliment," she argues.

Sam snickers, and honestly, I don't know why I would've expected anything different from them.

But I'm smart enough to not put them on speaker. And for that same reason, I didn't do a video call. Which is good because I'm sure the redness of my cheeks would give away my thoughts. Because really, I can't hear someone talk about Michael's dick and not blush. Especially since I know they're talking about the hot tub photo.

A photo I've saved to my phone and looked at more than a few times.

I really hope when Michael finds the photographer, he can get the uncensored versions.

"Okay, but for real." Sam finally speaks up. "Are you okay? The photos are obviously super hot, but I'm guessing you guys didn't plant them."

Michael snaps something into his phone as he paces through the open double doors leading from where I am in the bedroom out to the living room part of the suite.

"Yeah, no. We didn't plant them." I keep my voice down. "Michael is furious. Mostly on my behalf, it seems."

My cousins make matching sounds of intrigue.

"I can see why a man like Michael wouldn't want the world seeing his woman with a mouthful of d—"

"Sam!" I can't help my laugh. "You are so crass."

She snorts. "You know I'm right though."

"You are." I sigh. "And it's not exactly a great look for him. Or the show." I bite my lip. "Speaking of which…"

I don't know if it's supposed to be a secret, but considering the show starts airing tomorrow, it's not like it can be a secret for long.

Michael holds his phone in front of him, hanging up his call, then starts a new one.

"What about the show?" Sam asks.

"Well, Pamela got sick and now she can't make it. So." I take a deep breath. "I'm going to judge alongside Michael."

The two of them shriek.

I pull the phone away from my ear and wait for the shrill noise to die down.

"It's bonkers," I say when they're quiet enough to hear me again.

"It's fucking awesome." Suzy sounds like she might be crying.

"It's fucking something," I mumble, still not sure I'll be any good at it.

"I can hear that self-doubt in your tone," Sam chides. "Stop that right now."

I roll my eyes. "Thanks, Mom."

She makes a sound. "I take it the show isn't mad about the pictures?"

"Surprisingly, no. They seem to think it will be good for ratings." I shake my head even though they can't see it. "Seems a little backward to me, but what do I know."

"Drama sells and all that, I guess." Suzy hums.

"Yeah, I guess." I shrug.

"So, is Michael trying to find the photographer, or is he just letting it go?"

I watch Michael pace some more, his free hand clenched at his side.

"I think he said something about hiring a private investigator," I tell them. "But I'm not really sure how all that works."

Suzy whistles. "Me either. But it's cool to have PI money. And if anyone can hunt the fucker down, my bet is on HDM."

I groan. "Do I even want to know what that stands for?"

"Oh, let me guess!" Sam sounds like she's bouncing on her toes.

"Sam," Suzy says like she's calling on her.

"What is Huge Dick Michael."

"Ding, ding! Got it in one!" Suzy cheers.

I do my best not to laugh. "I'm hanging up now."

"Bye! Good luck!" Sam tells me.

"With the dick," Suzy adds.

"And be careful," Sam warns.

"With the dick," Suzy repeats, laughing at her own joke.

"Oh my god, bye." I hang up.

Setting my phone on the bed next to me, I have to admit I feel a little lighter, even if my cousins are ridiculous.

Michael paces back in my direction, and his features soften once his gaze lifts and meets mine.

"As soon as you know, I know," he says to the person on the other end of the line, then hangs up.

I stay put, letting him cross the space to me.

"How are your cousins?" Michael nods to my phone.

"Ridiculous," I answer. "Did you talk to the investigator guy?"

Michael nods.

"What did he say?" I cross my legs, making room for Michael.

He lowers himself to sit on the edge of the bed, facing me. "Said he'll start right away."

"Oh wow." My brows lift. "Will he go to the cabin? I don't actually know how this works."

Michael shrugs. "He might end up going, but he sounded confident he could find the identity of the photographer digitally."

"Oh." My shoulders lower.

"Don't sound so disappointed." Michael chuckles. "It will still take detective work. And once he finds the guy who took the pictures, he can find out if anyone put him up to it."

I make a humming sound. "I dunno. That picture of your ass was pretty well framed. It might have been a woman who took them."

Michael gives me a deadpan look, and I only last a second before I crack and laugh.

"Fine." I concede. "You're right, it was probably a man because men are the worst."

Michael dips his chin. "Precisely."

"But what do you mean 'put him up to it'? Weren't we rerouted in the middle of the flight? How would anyone know where to find us?"

"These people can work quickly. And there was an entire

plane full of people who knew we were snowed in somewhere near Bear Cove. Even with the last-minute rental, the options were pretty limited, so it wouldn't have been hard for someone to find us."

I scrunch up my nose. "And what, someone went out in the storm searching for a place with the lights on just to take some photos?"

Michael reaches out and takes my hands in his. "Most people aren't like this. I want you to know that."

His tone is so apologetic, and I scoot closer.

I flex my fingers in his. "I know."

He squeezes mine back. "If I thought there was any chance that someone would do... what they did, I'd have kept you inside with all the curtains pulled shut."

I scoot another inch closer until our knees touch. "Underneath the covers, just to be safe?"

His sigh is half humor, half frustration. "I really am sorry, Alice. This isn't the way I wanted to introduce you to fame. My fans are better than this."

"Please don't apologize. You didn't take the photos. You didn't, what, sell them?" I tilt my head, thinking about it. "How much do you think those pictures sold for?"

He shrugs. "Something scandalous like that? Probably ten grand an image. Maybe more. Maybe a lot more."

That amount of money might not seem like much to Michael, but it makes me want to gag.

"Do you have to buy them back?" Our talk from earlier is fresh in my mind. The one where I admitted to having basically no money, and the urge to gag gets stronger. We both know I can't help pay for it if that's what he has to do.

Michael shakes his head as he runs his thumbs over my wrists. "There's no point. The tabloid is the one that bought them, they got the scoop and the initial major spike in views, but the photos are online now. There's no stopping them."

I slide one of my hands free from his grip and press it to my stomach. "You seem very calm about this."

This being the half dozen photos of us, in the middle of various sex acts, plastered all over the internet.

Michael leans forward, stopping when his nose is just inches from mine. "I'm not okay with it. I'm not okay with the comments and bullshit you're going to have to deal with. And I'm really not okay with all my relatives knowing what my bare ass looks like."

I bite down on a smile. "I didn't think about that."

"I'm trying not to. But I'm glad it was my ass and not yours. Because your naughty bits are just for me." Michael rolls up onto his knees and pushes me onto my back. "And as much as I don't want anyone else to know what your face looks like when you come, I'm glad the world knows you're mine."

I reach for him. "Michael."

With me flat on my back, Michael drops his weight over me. "And I don't like that people know what you look like with a dick in your mouth. But I do like how greedily you swallowed me down."

My legs spread on their own, and Michael's arousal presses against my center.

I roll my hips and whisper his name this time.

He rocks into me. "So, to answer your question, I'm not calm, Sweetness." He rocks his hips again. "I'm not calm at all."

He lowers his face.

His lips a breath away from mine.

And then someone knocks on the door.

MICHAEL

*M*y nostrils flare as I try to tamp down my annoyance.

I'm usually good at controlling my emotions. Or at least keeping them off my face. But this rollercoaster of a day has been a fucking struggle.

The drop of depression at having to leave that little cottage when all I wanted to do was stay there, in bed, with my woman,

The spike of rage at finding those photos, on display, in the fucking airport.

The lust at examining the photos.

The satisfied joy at learning Alice will be my co-judge on the show.

And now the feel of Alice's soft body beneath mine, but not being able to take out my frustration by filling her in every way I can think of because—the noise sounds again—someone is knocking on our fucking hotel door.

I roll off Alice with a sexually frustrated groan and stomp across the suite.

"Wait!" Alice calls after me, and I hear her feet slapping

against the floor as she chases after me. "You can't answer the door like that!"

She grips my wrist.

"Like what?" I growl, not angry with her, just the situation.

She doesn't flinch at my tone. Instead she snickers. "Like that."

Alice reaches out with her free hand, and I jolt when she cups my dick through my pants.

My cock throbs, reminding me that I'm hard, and it's obvious.

"You're not answering the door alone," I tell her, trying not to lean into her touch.

"And I'm not letting the world see any more of your dick than they already have," she retorts.

I take a slow breath, trying to calm said dick, but it's impossible with the heat of her hand against me.

"Fine." I concede. "You can stand in front of me."

She rolls her eyes but steps ahead of me.

There's a third knock at the door.

"Fucking chill," I snap. "We're coming."

Alice mutters something that sounds like *I wish*, but I purposely ignore her. If I start imagining her coming on my dick, it will never deflate.

ALICE

I swing the door open, then have to jump back when a rolling clothing rack fills the doorway.

"Sorry, coming through!" a woman hidden by the clothes shouts.

Michael's big hands land on my shoulders, and he pulls me off to the side.

He keeps my body in front of his, and I have to stop myself from grinning.

The rack stops, and a pretty woman in her thirties steps out from behind it.

"Hi," she greets. "I'm G, from wardrobe."

A cool name to go with a cool job. And as much as I want to cheer her on for being a boss beauty, I no longer feel like grinning over Michael's boner. If she sees his bulge, I'm going to strangle her with a pair of expensive trousers.

"Hello." I say it quieter than I mean to. "I'm Alice."

"Oh, I know who you are, babe." G winks.

My cheeks heat.

I've never had another woman call me *babe* before.

"Hey, Chef Mike."

"Hi, G," he replies from behind me.

"You really know how to rile up the press, huh?" G snickers, and I'm back to not liking her.

Thankfully, G doesn't say more, just turns to her rack and starts pulling items off.

She has a man's button-down shirt in black and dark wash jeans slung over her arm when she turns around.

"For you." She holds them out for Michael. "I'll check the fit when you have them on, then I want you in the all-black sneakers."

Michael steps around me to take the clothes, and I keep my gaze focused above his belt, not wanting to draw attention to his lower half in case he's still... aroused.

Clothes tucked under his arm, Michael starts to pull his shirt free from his jeans.

"Nope," I bite out and point across the suite. "You change in the bedroom. With the door closed."

I watch him as he tries not to smile. "Yes, ma'am."

I don't look away until the bedroom door clicks shut behind him.

When I turn back to G, she has the biggest smile on her face. "Damn. I don't know which of you I'm more in love with."

"Um..." Having zero clue how to answer that statement, I move my gaze to the clothes. "Are those really for me to wear?"

G spins back to the rack. "Yep." She pulls a pair of navy wide-leg slacks off a hanger, followed by a silver silky long-sleeved top. "I'm pretty good at eyeballing sizes, and I tried to get a feel for your style by rewatching your episodes."

"Oh." I try not to sound horrified at the idea of someone watching the show specifically to figure out my dress size.

She faces me. "Did you and Chef Mike really meet there? Or did you know each other before?"

"We met on the show."

I'm not sure if there are things we're supposed to say or not say, so I figure short answers are best.

"That's so adorable." G makes a show of sighing. "You two were so... amazing." She lifts one of her hands and fans herself. "And the chemistry was off the charts."

"Uh, thanks." God, I sound as uncomfortable as I feel.

G glances at her watch. "Shit, sorry, we're running behind. Gonna need you to try these on." She thrusts the clothes at me. "This is the one I think will fit best, but I have it in a size up and down if you don't like the feel."

I take the items of clothing and peek at the tag, surprised to see it's the size I'd usually buy. Also surprised she was able to find such pretty items on such short notice.

From my experience, most department stores don't have good plus-size options, let alone have them in stock.

"Are you wearing a thong?" G asks.

I blink at her. "Yes."

She dips her chin. "Good. Panty lines aren't great for promo."

"Wait, what is this for?" I hold up the clothing. I assumed it was just for us to wear tomorrow.

It's G's turn to blink. "Promo. You'll wear it for the first episode too, but we have a photo shoot in five minutes. So strip."

"Five?" I squeak and forget all about being shy as I drop the clothes onto the couch, and then, standing in the middle of the living room area, I shove my pants down.

She can't see Michael undressed, but I don't really care if she sees me.

I'm bent over, pulling my pants free, when I hear the bedroom door open behind me.

There's a curse.

Then the door shuts again.

G snorts a laugh.

And I hope the day can only get better from here.

MICHAEL

*W*hen Alice stands from the hair and makeup chair, it takes all my will power not to stride directly to her and slam my mouth to hers.

But I don't do that.

Because I have *some* self-control.

Also because her makeup looks perfectly applied, and I won't be responsible for messing it up.

As she nears, the bright lights shine across her features, and I notice how glossy her lips are.

So glossy they're almost obscene.

But maybe that's just me, picturing her in the hot tub, with my cum dripping off her mouth.

I clear my throat as she stops before me. "You look beautiful."

Alice beams. "You look pretty handsome yourself."

"Alright, lovebirds." A new woman, this one with a still camera, snaps her fingers. "Let's get this literal show on the road."

ALICE

$\mathcal{W}$e follow the photographer's directions as she has us stand in various locations and poses on the set.

It's surreal to be back on the *Second Bite* set. Or rather, the traveling version, not the actual set out in California.

When I first walked out between the workstations back in Minnesota, I knew it would be a life-changing experience. I knew I'd never be the same.

And now…

Now I'm back on set.

In Canada.

With Michael.

As a freaking judge!

"Finally." The camerawoman huffs.

Wondering what we're doing wrong, I jerk my gaze over to the photographer, but she's talking to Joey, who's striding across the room toward us.

"Come over here." She points at me and Michael.

Joey continues to saunter, unbothered by her tone.

He's been the host of *Second Bite* for years, so he's probably used to the bossiness of some of the crew.

He's not as popular as Michael, but he's good looking and outgoing, as TV hosts usually are.

"Hey, Alice. How nice to see you again." His smile tells me he's seen the photos, and I feel myself blushing again.

I really need to just accept that every human on Earth has probably seen the photos and deal with it.

"Mike." Joey tips his head at Michael.

Michael grunts in reply.

"Joey." The photographer snaps her fingers. "Stand between these two."

I start to step away from Michael to make room, but a hand clamps down on my shoulder.

"No." Michael's gruff tone leaves no room for argument.

The photographer sighs but doesn't complain, just directs Joey to stand a few inches to my right.

Michael stays plastered to my left side, his arm still draped across my shoulders, and I can totally picture him stretching his hand out, shoving Joey away if he gets too close.

Placing my hand in the middle of Michael's back, I look up at him.

As expected, his face is set in a scowl, and I bite my lip in an attempt to keep my smile under control.

There's a flash.

"Perfect. Hold that."

Me?

I look over at the photographer.

"Alice. Stop moving." She bites the words out.

My mouth pops open, embarrassment flooding my cheeks.

There's another flash.

Joey chuckles at my side, and I turn my head to look at him.

Apparently not liking that, Michael tightens his hold on me, forcing my body to aim toward his even as I look over my shoulder at Joey.

Another fucking flash.

THE COUSINS WON'T STOP SENDING me audio clips of themselves laughing.

For some reason, I thought the promo photos would take longer to be posted. As in, maybe tomorrow morning before the first episode. I was not expecting them to go viral an hour after we finished shooting them.

The pictures are pretty entertaining. And even though I'm the one who looks ridiculous, I can see why they used them.

There are a few of just Michael and me, but the three photos of us with Joey are popping up everywhere.

Me gazing at Michael, every bit of my love for him obvious in my expression.

Me with my mouth and eyes wide open, looking guilty as hell pressed into Michael's side.

And me hugged against Michael's body, looking over my shoulder at Joey, who's smirking at both of us.

I didn't look at the online comments.

I'm not interested in hurting my own feelings.

But my cousins sent me screenshots of the best ones.

Anyone else still just thinking about that hot tub picture?

Fuck me, I hope they have babies immediately.

Would pay so much money to see Chef Mike punch Joey in the face for looking too closely at his girl.

We all pretending we wouldn't prefer an episode of Naked Bite?

Back in pajamas, I drop onto the bed.

After the photo shoot, we came up to our room, and I carefully removed my clothes, making sure to smooth out any wrinkles as I hung them up.

Michael said he had to run out to take care of something, probably tabloid related, so I put on my pajamas and ordered room service.

Tomorrow is the first day of filming, and as much as I want to be at Michael's side, I don't know anything that would help out in the investigation.

I shimmy under the covers.

I don't want to go to sleep without Michael, so I'll wait up for him. But I can just rest my eyes.

MICHAEL

Nodding, I sign the slip of paper in front of me. "I need it in two days."

The jeweler's eyes widen. "Two?"

I set the pen down. "Two."

ALICE

*S*omething beeps.

Then beeps again.

My eyes pop open.

My brain feels scrambled, trying to remember where we are, as I start to sit up.

But then a heavy arm tugs me back down.

"Snooze it, Baby." Michael's voice is scratchy.

"What?" My own voice comes out wonky.

The beeping continues, and I connect the dots.

Reaching out, I slap my hand around on the nightstand until I find my phone.

It goes silent.

"Sorry, I meant to stay up." I rub my eyes. I'd really only meant to close them for a moment, but the light around the edges of the closed curtains tells me that moment was about seven hours.

"You needed the rest." Michael yawns as he says it, and I smile. "Now close your eyes and hush."

My smile turns into a grin. "So grumpy in the morning."

He grunts in reply.

I pat the arm that's over me. "I'm going to shower. If I fall back asleep, I'll just have stress dreams about being late."

"Fine," Michael groans. "Abandon me."

I lean over and kiss his cheek, then wiggle out of bed.

Today is the first day of the New Year's Special. And like the holiday special I was a contestant on, this one is also live streamed. Which means I need to find the right caffeine level between alert and sprinting to the bathroom.

"PLACES, EVERYONE!"

Oh god, oh god, oh god.

"We're going live in three... two..." The man behind the camera holds up a single finger. The big light in the front of the room flashes red. And my heart stops.

How is this even worse the second time around?

But unlike the first time, I'm at the front of the room, and Michael is flexing his fingers around mine.

I take a breath and feel a little calmer as I squeeze his fingers back.

Michael will be at my side, literally, through every step of the show.

I can do this.

Joey starts his usual introduction to the show, and I finally realize that the four workbenches in front of us are empty.

When we did the holiday show last week, the four of us were at our benches before the cameras went live.

That's weird.

"And we have a few special treats for you today, no pun intended." Joey chuckles at his joke. "First, judging alongside her beau, Chef Mike, we have the lovely Alice Hatter joining us." He sweeps an arm out in my direction.

Reminding myself this is live, I give my best smile. "Thanks, Joey. I'm excited to be on this side of the apron today." Then I remember why I'm here in the first place. "But, uh, wishing Pamela a speedy recovery."

I have a second of panic as I wonder if her illness is supposed to be a secret, but then Joey nods his head.

"I talked to Pamela this morning, and she's confident she'll be sipping champagne by the New Year." Joey moves around to Michael's side, continuing the intro to the show. "And, of course, we have the one and only Chef Mike, who we all know is *healthy* like a horse."

He emphasizes the word healthy, and I have to work to keep my expression even.

Joey can't possibly be alluding to the term *hung like a horse* on live TV.

Could he?

I didn't think to ask anyone about the... pictures. I just assumed no one would make any jokes or comments. That we would all pretend it never happened.

Michael doesn't react. He just does what he always does during the intro. He gives a silent nod to the camera.

Except it's not the same as always because Michael usually has his arms crossed while he mean mugs. But today he can't. Because he's holding my hand.

"And the second surprise today..." Joey drums his hands on his thighs. "To celebrate the New Year right, all our contestants are celebrities!"

Celebrities?

"Oh hell," I think I say.

Then I sway.

MICHAEL

*a*lice's grip loosens on mine, and she starts to lean lazily away from me.

Spinning toward her, I grip her shoulders.

"Alice." I hold her steady. "Look at me. Are you okay?"

She blinks.

"Alice," I say sternly.

"Sorry. Sorry. I'm okay." Alice glances around. "The surprise was surprising." She tries to laugh.

"Dammit, Baby Cakes." I huff out a breath. "You took a damn year off my life. Are you sure you're okay?"

"Totally fine." She leans around me to lift a hand at one of the camera guys. "Just excited for the contestants."

Someone on set chuckles.

Sighing, I slide my hands down her arms, then move back to her side.

"That was fun. Alrighty." Joey grins at us. "Chef Mike and Baby Cakes, you ready to meet your contestants?"

I want to strangle him for daring to call her that. But shouting at him during a live-stream episode will only ensure that everyone will call her that. And it was my fault for saying it. So instead of inflicting bodily harm, I just stare daggers at Joey.

"Um, yes, please." Alice's answer is soft, but our body mics are sensitive, so they pick up every little sound.

Joey turns toward a door at the far side of the spacious room. "It's my pleasure to introduce the four celebrities competing this weekend. First up, we have the Oscar-winning actor, and stealer of hearts, Drake Daniels."

The door opens, and I recognize the man who steps through.

Drake walks up to the first workstation, the one closest to us, and grins. "Pleasure to be here."

I've watched some of his action movies. He's a good actor.

He's also known for being very good looking.

I squeeze Alice's hand. My silent warning for her not to stare at him.

"Next." Joey pauses as the door opens again. "We have Colby Canterbury. Stand-up comedian with a no-longer-secret knack for baking."

Colby stops at the table across from Drake. "Jokes and yokes. I'm here to serve both."

I've heard of this guy but have never seen his act.

I'm annoyed they're springing this celebrity shit on us without warning. I'm not just the talent, this *is my* show. I should know about things like this. Not only so I can be prepared, but so I can vet the guests. Make sure no one is problematic. Make sure they don't choose someone I have an issue with.

I bite back the urge to growl.

So far the contestants are fine, but I'm still gonna have someone's neck later.

"Baker number three is the talented and brilliant Canadian pop singer, Zelle," Joey announces, and Alice gasps.

A short woman with long brown hair moves to the bench behind Drake. "Hello."

"Oh my god, I love her so much," Alice whispers beside me.

I have to fight my smile. The contestants can't hear her, but her sentiment is still being live streamed. I'll have to remind Alice tonight that every word is picked up and just hope she doesn't say anything sexy to me before the end of the challenge.

"Last but never least." Joey lifts a hand toward the door. "Amber Addison."

My head snaps over to look at Joey.

He says something about Amber being a popular soap opera actress.

Mentions something else.

But I'm not listening. Just watching.

Joey doesn't look any different than usual.

Isn't acting like a guilty man.

Isn't acting like anything is wrong.

So maybe he doesn't know.

But someone knew, and inwardly, I seethe as my ex-girl-friend walks to the fourth and final workbench.

The redhead lifts her hand. "Hi, Joey. It's so good to be here."

ALICE

I'm going to hyperventilate.

This is too much.

Drake reaches across the table and shakes my hand.

Drake doesn't do it for me anymore. Michael is the only one with the keys to my gift box now, but everyone in the world finds Drake attractive.

I think I'm supposed to say something, ask something, but all I can do is smile at Drake.

Michael moves his hand to the center of my back, and I let go of Drake's hand.

"What are you making for today's challenge?" Michael asks.

Drake smiles that lopsided smile he's famous for. "Lemon and ginger cake."

As he starts to talk about the ingredients, I let myself remember all the episodes of *Second Bite* that I've watched over and over again.

I know how to do this.

I know how this is supposed to go.

And as we move on, I get into the swing of it.

I ask the questions.

Hum at *hopefully* the right times.

And do my best not to scrunch my nose when Colby tells us he's making a tomato cake.

Michael seems to know what it is and is excited about trying it, but I think it sounds disgusting.

We talk to Zelle, and I have to stop myself from leaning down and resting my chin on her work top because her talking voice is just as pretty as her singing voice, and I could listen to her all day.

Not to mention, she's just as pretty in person. I know the trolls online are always making comments about her weight, but I just think it's awesome to see such a successful artist who's my size.

"Good luck," Michael tells Zelle, then I swear he grumbles as Joey leads us to the final contestant.

I try so hard to keep my smile normal, but seriously, how can I? I'm about to meet Amber Addison!

The queen of soap operas.

The master of the instant cry.

The woman who was basically my babysitter after school for years.

We stop before her, and I'm beaming like a fool.

But Amber doesn't look at me. "Hello, Michael."

My smile dims.

Michael. Only his close friends and family call him that.

"Hello." Michael's tone is sharp and causes me to look up at him.

If someone didn't know him well, maybe they wouldn't catch the difference. But I can hear it. He's tense.

Joey clears his throat, familiar enough with Michael's habits.

Trying to remain unaffected by whatever is happening, I hold my hand out to Amber. "Hi, it's so great to meet you."

Her beautifully crafted eyebrows lift as she turns her head to look at me.

She takes my hand, not saying anything.

"I'm a big fan," I tell her honestly. "I've been watching you on *Dawns of Agony* since I was a kid."

Amber narrows her eyes. "That's nice."

Her tone is icy, and I worry that what I said came off as insulting when I meant it as a compliment.

She drops my hand and turns to Michael. "I'm going to make an orange spice cake. It might be cheating since it's the recipe you taught me, but at least I know you'll like it."

The recipe you taught me.

Is this bitch implying what I think she's implying?

"So, uh, I take it you two know each other?" Joey asks the question that's thudding inside my skull.

Amber lets out something that I would have called a tinkling laugh a moment ago, but to me she sounds like a braying donkey. "I mean, if dating counts as knowing each other."

Dating.

She dated Michael?

How?

How could I not know that?

"When was that?" Joey asks, sounding as stunned by this information as I am.

"Oh, probably back when *this one* was a kid." She waves a hand in my direction.

This. Old. Bitch.

"Isn't that right, Michael?" Amber reaches out like she's going to touch Michael's arm.

And hand to the cookie gods, I swear time slows around me.

I can hear every heartbeat.

I can feel her exhaled breath as she chuckles.

And I summon lightning through the ceiling. It zaps Amber, and she lights up like a cartoon x-ray. Her full skeleton on display. Her heart nothing but a pile of chewed-on chicken bones.

A large palm grips the back of my neck just as I start to lean forward.

Michael tightens his fingers, keeping me from lunging at this hag.

Teeth clenched, I glance up at him.

His mouth is flat, but his eyes are on fire. And I see he's put his other hand in his pants pocket, keeping it out of Amber's reach.

The knowledge settles me. Just a little.

"Welp." Joey claps once. "Good luck with your cake."

Fuck this lady and her cake. I want to shove those oranges up her nose.

Michael uses his hold on my neck to steer me away from the source of my fury.

Away from Amber fucking Addison.

MICHAEL

*A*lice is practically vibrating under my palm, and I hate that she's upset. Hate that this is happening to her on live TV.

But... I kind of love that she's full of jealousy.

Which is understandable, even if there are zero feelings between me and Amber. Because if the assholes in charge dared to bring one of her ex-boyfriends onto my show, I'd bake him into a six-foot calzone.

"Mi—" Alice starts to say my name, and I flex my fingers against her neck as I guide her away from the contestants.

The clock is ticking on the New Year's fruitcake challenge, and there's no stopping it. So for the next hour and a half, we just have to sit up at the front of the large room, in view of the cameras.

But we won't have to talk to Amber again until judging.

Fucking Amber.

What the fuck were the producers thinking?

Our relationship was never public. Hardly even a relationship. But someone had to know. There's no possible way this happened just by chance.

"Michael," Alice hisses under her breath.

"Baby," I whisper back.

Her eyes are narrowed up at me. "Don't you *Baby* me. Did you—"

This time I cut her off by turning her toward me and gripping her chin.

I mouth the word *don't.*

If she asks me if I knew about this, I'm going to lose it.

I get it.

This is fucked.

I can't even really blame her for wanting to ask it.

But I still hate it. Because she knows me better than that.

Instead of going to the two director's chairs set up for us, I let go of Alice's chin and aim her toward one of the free-standing refrigerators.

I swear I can hear her mouth open, probably to hiss something else at me, so I rush the final few steps.

I put her back against the back of the fridge and crowd into her space.

We're making a scene. There's no way the cameras won't follow us. But I just need to remind her about these fucking microphones and hope she's willing to wait until we get upstairs to discuss this.

I point to my chest, where the small mic is attached to my shirt, next to one of my buttons.

She heaves out a breath. "I know." I start to relax. "You're my Mr. Claus and in charge, but this…"

My moment of relaxation ends.

Alice waves a hand back toward the contestants, and I don't know if I want to slap my hand to my face or burst out laughing.

"Alice," I say it as quietly as I can.

"But she's seen the photos of me suck—"

I slam my mouth to hers.

My lips cut off the rest of her words. Words that I just know were going to be *sucking your dick.*

Alice's body instantly softens into mine, all her tension vanishing against my lips.

And I want to deepen the kiss.

Want to lift her and shove her against the fridge.

Want to bury myself inside her and remind her that she's my one and only.

But we're on live TV.

I pull back, and before she can make that little whiny sound that goes straight to my balls, I press my finger to her lips.

Her eyes are narrowed again, but this time it's because she wants more kisses, not because she's angry with me.

I slowly remove my finger, then bring it directly to the mic on my shirt.

She follows the movement.

Then her gaze jumps back up to meet mine.

I nod once. And mouth *every word.*

Her mouth parts in an O as she finally understands.

Then her eyes widen, probably remembering what she said right before I kissed her.

I nod again, and even though the whole situation is a mess, I can't stop my smile.

Alice reaches out and places a palm over my mic and then one over her own.

"You still love me the most, right?" She whispers it so quietly that it's only for my ears.

She's smiling. But it's a soft smile. One with a hint of insecurity.

I grip her wrists and pull her hands off the mics.

"I'll always love you the most."

ALICE

"Wow." I hold my hand over my mouth as I say it.

I'm not even mad that Amber made this. How can I be mad when this is the fourth cake I've tasted, and each has been just as delicious as the last? Even that weird-ass tomato cake.

Michael nods as he takes a bite.

After spending the challenge time sitting beside Michael while the bakers baked, I was able to look past my own tension to see his. And as much as I hate that his ex was somehow put on the show, I don't want my man to have to deal with a woman he doesn't like. And if that means taking the lead on this tasting, so be it.

"Seriously." I keep going because fuck, this c-word can bake. "I don't care where the recipe came from, the cake is moist and light. You managed to keep the orange flavor bright. And even with the cinnamon glaze, it still feels fresh." I pick up one of the mini stars covered in edible glitter. "And these little spiced cookies are the perfect touch for New Year's."

I pop the cookie in my mouth and find Amber Addison gaping at me.

I pull my shoulders back a bit more as pride fills me.

Take that, soap opera writers! I know how to throw down a plot twist when necessary.

"Yes, well." Amber blinks back her composure. "It's always been a *pleasure* to make in the past."

"I bet," I answer cheerily as I pop another star cookie into my mouth.

I know what she's trying to do.

And I want to pour the rest of her glitter into my hand, then blow it into her face for saying the word pleasure like that in front of *my* Michael.

But I'll settle for moaning around my mouthful while I soak in the feeling of Michael setting his hand on my shoulder.

I don't miss the way Amber watches the movement.

And I don't miss the way her eye twitches.

And I certainly don't miss the fact that Michael is keeping his hand where it is, making no move to lift his fork for a second bite.

MICHAEL

When the cameras shut off, I don't waste any time. Alice turns like she's going to go talk to someone, but I grab her hand to stop her.

I use my other hand to point at the producer about to walk past. "I'll be back down to talk to you." My tone tells him it isn't going to be a friendly talk, and I'm sure it's no mystery what I'm pissed about.

He nods, and I turn away.

Alice doesn't argue or ask where we're going when I start to tug her along with me.

She did amazing today.

Better than amazing. She was fucking perfect. A total natural.

But I know it cost her.

Playing nice and complimenting Amber had to cost her.

Just like in Minneapolis, the *Second Bite* set is in a large ball-room inside the same hotel everyone is staying in. Including us.

The elevator bay is blessedly empty as I stride straight over and press the up button.

"Is there anything else we have to do?" Alice asks, just as an elevator opens behind her. "Or are we done?"

I crowd her backward through the open doors. "We're never gonna be done, Little Sweetness."

She clutches at my shirt. "You know that's not what I meant."

"I know." I pause just long enough to hit the button for our floor. "But I need more of your sweet words right now."

I press her against the back wall of the elevator.

"Sweet words?" Her chest heaves against mine.

"Yeah, Baby. That's why you're my Sweetness. My Sweet Girl. It's not just that candy slit between your legs that makes you so sweet. It's the words that come out of your mouth. It's your words that make me feel so fucking good."

Instead of giving me those words, Alice brings her hands up and grips my neck.

Her eyes are bright while she pulls my face down to meet hers.

And I let her.

My mouth fuses with hers, and I finally get to kiss her the way I've wanted to since this morning.

I push my tongue past her lips.

And she sucks it.

Alice sucks my tongue into her mouth as her nails claw against the back of my neck, and I feel the shape of her settle into my heart.

Every day.

Every day, for the rest of my life, I'm going to come home to this woman.

I wrap my arms around her and hoist her into the air.

Alice lets out a sound of surprise, but when I boost her up, her face becomes level with mine, and she deepens the kiss.

A groan rumbles through my chest when Alice tightens her legs around my waist.

I hear the doors slide open behind me, and I turn, Alice still wrapped around me.

There's a startled yelp from someone who isn't us. And a person blurs past us into the elevator as we exit.

This is hardly more illicit than what the world has already seen, so I decide it doesn't matter that they saw us.

I shift my grip on Alice and get the room key out of my pocket, fumbling for a moment to get the door open.

It slams shut behind us.

And the bedroom is too far away.

I aim for the living room, and when my knees bump against the couch, I drop my girl.

She bounces once with a little puff of an exhale.

I kneel before her.

"Pants off." My demand is hardly necessary since I'm already pulling her zipper down and Alice is already lifting her hips.

I tug them off, thong and all.

"Michael." Alice reaches for me.

I evade her grasp and lower my face between her thighs. "Talk to me, Baby Cakes. Give me those sweet words."

"I don't—" Alice cuts off on a gasp as I press my tongue to her entrance and lick.

ALICE

$\mathcal{M}$ichael is devouring me like I'm his dessert and he hasn't eaten four cakes already today.

A finger presses into me, and electricity zips through my belly.

"Oh my Chef," I breathe.

Words. He wants my words.

But I don't know what to say.

"My-my Love." I reach down and grip his hair. "You're so good to me. I love you so much."

I feel foolish the moment I say it. This isn't good dirty talk. But then Michael moans against my pussy. The vibrations rattle against my clit, and I suddenly don't feel so foolish anymore.

"You're even better than all my fantasies put together." I tell him the truth as he laps at me. "I feel so lucky to have you."

Michael shakes his head, his lips rubbing against my pussy as he does it.

I smile through the bliss.

"I'd feel even luckier," I pant, "if you'd put that big dick of yours inside me now."

Michael's tongue pulls away from my core as he sits up on

249

his knees. "See what a sweet mouth you have?" He reaches down and opens the front of his pants. "And if my Baby Cakes wants to be full of my dick, then that's exactly what she'll get."

I spread my legs wider. "Yes, please."

Michael shoves the front of his boxer briefs down and grips his cock. "Keep talking, Sweetness." He notches the tip of his dick against my entrance. "I want to hear those pretty words until you come."

Michael grips my hips and jerks me toward him as he slams his hips forward.

MICHAEL

*A*lice cries out, and I have to close my eyes.

Heat surrounds me, and the way Alice's body is clenching around my length is nearly enough to send me over the edge.

"You're so handsome," she chants, "so strong."

I slide my eyes open as I pull my hips back.

The way Alice talks is so fucking innocent, and yet it's lighting me on fire.

I rock forward and bring a hand between us, pressing my thumb to her clit.

Alice jolts at the contact, and her eyes—which had lowered to where we're joined—snap up to meet mine.

"More," I demand as I start to circle my thumb.

"I love your hands." She clutches at the cushion beneath her. "Your fingers are so big."

"These fingers?" I ask, slipping the middle finger of my free hand through her slickness. "Think you can take both?"

With her head propped up against the back of the couch, Alice looks to where my hands are.

I flatten my hand on her stomach so she can see better, but I keep my thumb where it is, working her clit.

"You want me to shove this finger inside you too?" I ask, wiggling my finger at her entrance against the top of my cock.

I've never done this before, but now that I have Alice, I want to try everything.

Alice's lips part, but she just nods.

I pull back so my dick is almost all the way out, then I slide the tip of my finger along the top of my cock until it's against her heat.

Then I slowly push forward, sliding my dick and finger into her heat at the same time.

"Tell me how it feels," I grit out.

"Good. Oh god, it feels so good." Her hips wriggle as she attempts to pull me deeper. "I feel so full, Michael."

I push both in as far as they'll go.

Alice moans.

I pull out.

Push in.

We create a rhythm.

Alice tightens around me as she gets closer.

I keep moving and rubbing her little clit.

"My Chef." She squeezes her eyes shut. "My Michael."

"That's right, my Alice." I feel my orgasm building. "Taking all of me so well. Now come on my cock and prove you're mine,"

I press my finger inside her pussy as I jiggle her clit, and she bursts.

Her body is writhing, and I don't stop. I can't.

I keep rubbing her clit, and I keep thrusting inside her until it's all too much. Then I follow her over the edge.

ALICE

*M*ichael is waiting for me, sitting on the side of the bed, when I come out of the bathroom.

With no plans to leave the room, I've continued my tradition of pajamas by dinnertime and pulled my hair back.

I know he still wanted to go down and talk to the producers, so I'm not surprised to see him still dressed in his filming clothes, but I am surprised to see a room service cart next to him.

"Come here." He holds a hand out to me.

Not needing to be told twice, I move to him and step between his spread knees.

"Thank you for what you did today." His voice is full of so much compassion it makes my heart squeeze.

"You don't have to thank me." I take his offered hand and press my other palm over his heart.

"I do." He shakes his head and places his hand over mine, pinning it to his chest. "I didn't know Amber would be here." He presses his hand down harder, like he's worried I'll try to pull it away. "I don't know whose idea it was to bring her here, but their career with *Second Bite* is over."

"You don't—"

"I do," he says again. "Even if..." Michael swallows. "Even if I'd never met you, I'd still fire whoever brought her here. This show isn't about drama. It never should have happened. And certainly not with you, the love of my life, at my side."

"I'm mostly mad that I didn't know you two had dated. I thought I knew everything about you."

Michael's chest rises and falls with a deep breath. "It was twenty years ago. A lifetime ago. And I'll tell you whatever you want to know, but I hope you're okay knowing that it wasn't serious. It was casual and brief, and I would've thought her petty jealousy would've worn off by now. But she was dramatic back when I knew her, and she's already proven she's still dramatic now."

"Kind of have to be dramatic to be in soap operas." I pull a face. "I hate that meeting her has ruined *Dawns of Agony* for me. I watched that show after school like every day."

That gets a small smile out of Michael. "That was pretty perfect when you mentioned watching her when you were a kid. I know you weren't trying to needle her about her age, but it was pretty perfect anyway."

"I guess this is what they mean when they say never meet your heroes." I sigh. "Except Zelle is just as cool as I'd hoped she'd be." I bite my lip. "And Drake is really good looking."

Michael narrows his eyes.

"I'm kidding." I lean down and press a kiss to his lips.

"Better be," Michael grumbles.

"So... what did you order?" I eye the cart.

"A couple options for dinner. Whatever you don't eat, I'll have when I get back."

"I can wait for you."

Michael shakes his head. "After the producers, I need to call my manager. He should have at least known about the celebrity bit. The fact that I was completely in the dark, on my own show, is unacceptable."

I bite my lip.

"What?" Michael watches me.

"You're so hot when you're angry."

He shakes his head. "Go eat your food. I have to run out and grab a few things after my talks, so I'll be a bit."

After a hug and another quick kiss, Michael leaves the room.

Once he's gone, I select the burger from the options and pull out Michael's laptop. While I eat, I can watch the episode of *Dawns of Agony* when Amber's character dies in a freak collapsing-bookshelf accident.

ALICE

"*L*et's go to bed, Baby."

I blink into the dark room. "Bed?"

"Yeah, you fell asleep on the couch." Michael starts to tuck his hands under me like he's going to carry me, and I start to sit up. "Just wrap your arms around me."

Too tired to argue, I do as he says. And when he pulls me up off the couch, I wrap my legs around him.

It's just like earlier, him carrying me like this. Except this time, we're going to make it all the way to the bedroom.

I press my mouth to his shoulder to stifle my yawn.

"My sleepy little elf." Michael squeezes me tighter.

"You were gone a long time."

He slides one of his hands up and down my spine. "I know. I'm sorry."

I inhale him. "Why do you smell like vanilla?"

"I'm a baker, remember?"

I hum, my brain already drifting back to sleep, not thinking twice about his answer.

MICHAEL

"*H*ello and welcome to *Second Bite*," Joey says to the cameras. "We're on day two of our Celebrity New Year's Special. If you tuned in yesterday, you got to meet our contestants—Drake Daniels, Colby Canterbury, Zelle, and Amber Addison."

I can't even hear her name without feeling anger well inside me.

The producers all played dumb last night. Claiming they didn't know of the history between us, that casting had approved her application and they didn't think twice about it.

I mostly believe them. Though I'll keep digging.

At least my private investigator is competent.

He tracked down where the photo email originated from, and I can't say I'm surprised the location was Bear Cove, the town where the images were taken. So he's heading there today, and by tomorrow evening, I should know if it was someone working on their own, or if they were put up to the task.

"For today's challenge, you all must make a New Year's inspired ice cream dessert. Your dish must have—"

The static in my brain drowns out whatever Joey says next.

It's not supposed to be ice cream.

It's supposed to be cheesecake.

We did ice cream in the last special.

My eyes move to the back corner workstation.

To Amber.

She's looking right back at me, and the smile on her face might look casual to someone else, but I know her moods. She's up to something. And I have a feeling I know what that something is.

I just need Alice to hold her composure because I'm not sure I'll be able to.

ALICE

*Z*elle, the beautiful singer, bites her lips and nods. "Yep, a giant ice cream sandwich."

I grin at the idea and look over the ingredients on her workstation. "What flavors are you doing?"

"I really love the classic Neapolitan combination, so I'm sandwiching two vanilla sugar cookies with sprinkles"—she holds her hands out to demonstrate cookies the size of dinner plates—"around a strawberry ice cream, with finely diced fresh berries mixed in, along with dark chocolate shavings rather than the chips." Zelle lifts a shoulder. "I just think the shaved bits melt in your mouth better."

I press my lips together.

I press them together hard.

But it doesn't stop the snort.

Zelle blinks at me, then her blue eyes widen. "Oh god. I meant the chocolate."

I snort again and slap my hand over my mouth.

Michael shifts beside me, lifting his hand to the back of my neck. "It sounds lovely, Zelle. How thick do you expect it to be?"

I croak a laugh into my palm because, seriously?

"Pretty thick," Zelle squeaks as her cheeks turn red.

I feel like I might choke on the laughter I'm trying to hold back.

"Well, good luck." Joey cuts in, moving the show along like the professional he is.

Michael keeps his hand where it is, up under my hair, and I focus on the skin-on-skin contact as I catch my breath and prepare to face off with Amber the Asshole once again.

Joey gets to her bench first, greeting her with his usual happiness.

Amber replies, then turns to look at Michael, and only Michael, once again completely ignoring me.

"What are you doing?" Michael asks her flatly.

And I have to press my lips together again, only this time it's because he sounds so mad, and I can't help but find it arousing.

Amber blinks for a moment, like she was expecting him to be all friendly or something equally dumb, then her face morphs into a wide smile. "I'm making a chai ice cream."

Chai. Ice cream.

A red warning light flashes inside my brain.

She wouldn't...

"What else?" Michael's tone hasn't changed, and I realize he put it together long before we even got to the table.

And my new suspicion is confirmed when Amber replies. "A cinnamon filling."

Red starts to haze around my vision as indignation fills my chest.

Joey clears his throat. "And how are you presenting these items to make them New Year's themed?"

Still ignoring me, Amber turns to Joey. "Well, up here in Canada, New Year's is still winter, so I thought I'd put it all together into a snowman. Really celebrate the season."

"Okay..." Joey takes a step toward Michael, placing a hand

on his upper arm like he's getting ready to hold him back. "Good luck."

Before Amber can say anything else, Joey starts to push Michael away from Amber's workbench.

Michael steps into me, and it takes everything I have not to hold up my middle finger before I turn and walk away.

MICHAEL

"Very original presentation," I tell Drake as I cut a slice of the mocha-baked Alaska he made.

"Thank you." The man, who always looks so self-assured, looks a little nervous.

It never ceases to amaze me how insecure famous people can be when they have to do something outside their usual talent.

"Remind me of the layers," Alice asks him as I set half the slice onto her plate.

"There's a chocolate brownie base with a dome of coffee ice cream. And I added a touch of coconut into the meringue. I've found it gives it more of a marshmallow flavor."

Alice scoops up a bite and puts it in her mouth. "Holy Fu—" I nudge her with my elbow. "Fudgesicles."

Drake beams at her reaction, and as much as I don't want him smiling at my girl, I want her feeling as good as possible as we lead up to Amber.

I agree with Alice about the perfect balance of flavors and get the same giant smile in return.

We move through Colby's dessert. A grasshopper-mint ice

cream cake carved into the approximate shape of a champagne bottle, which is tasty even if the design is a bit rustic.

Zelle's giant ice cream sandwich, covered in silver and gold sprinkles, is just as delicious as I'd hoped. The strawberry and chocolate complement the sweetness of the sugar cookie.

And I'm glad the first three were amazing. Because I can't have Amber winning this competition. She proved herself a competent baker yesterday, and I still can't accept a world where Alice doesn't win on my show and Amber does.

But luckily for me, Amber has let her pettiness get the better of her, and it's going to be her downfall. Because one of the things we look at as judges is originality.

And there's nothing original about the cake she made yesterday, especially since she made a point to announce that it was one of my recipes.

And there's certainly nothing original about the dessert in front of her now.

I was thinking she would form her ice cream into spheres and build them into an actual snowman shape.

Figured she'd do something at least a little creative.

But the bitch has literally recreated Alice's ice cream snowman head. Down to the fondant carrot nose and black gingerbread hat.

The difference is the scarf. Instead of Alice's failed Jell-O scarf, which ultimately ruined her ice cream and chance of winning, Amber has created a scarf from red fondant and twisted it around the base of the snowman head.

I want to smash it with my fists.

Want to take a blow torch to it and melt it into a puddle.

The absolute fucking nerve of this woman.

How dare—

"Oh my god, it's perfect!" Alice exclaims.

Her voice is so cheerful it startles me out of my angry daze.

Alice starts to move at my side, and I keep my grip on the back of her neck but let her bend forward.

Amber's eyes lock on my arm, focusing on the fact that I'm touching Alice. That I'm not letting go.

But same as yesterday's judging, Amber doesn't seem to know how to handle Alice's compliments.

"This is seriously impressive." Alice inspects the snowman face a bit more, then straightens. "Exactly what I was going for when I made it last week."

Amber's smile falters.

And I have to resist my own.

I don't know why Amber is acting like the hurt party here. She wasn't even subtle about copying Alice. She did the exact same dessert that was aired just a handful of days ago. And she did it to shove it into Alice's face.

With my free hand, I slide the knife over to Alice. "Do the honors, Baby."

I probably shouldn't be using pet names during taping, but... I don't care.

Alice carves off two slices of the snowman head, and we try it at the same time.

I smile around the spoon.

It's delicious.

And it's Alice's recipe.

Alice moans too.

"Good?" Amber asks, her eyes on me.

"It is." I nod and set my spoon down. "But I hope you have plans to make something original tomorrow since your first two recipes have been remakes, and originality is one of the aspects we judge on."

Amber's smug look fades away.

I don't really want to give her a warning that she's fucked up. I'd love to shatter her little dreams of winning all at once. But when she doesn't win tomorrow, I need the audience to understand why. I can't have anyone questioning my decision, saying it was based off personal feelings. And after what I just said, the audience should be well aware that it's going to be a major long shot for her to win.

Alice grabs the knife again, and I worry for half a heartbeat that she's going to slash at Amber with it, but instead she slices off another chunk of the snowman's face.

"Sorry, gotta snag a bit more." She shrugs. "I really don't see myself making this ever again, even if it is delicious." Alice looks up at me. "I'll share if you'd like."

My admiration for this woman grows every second of every day.

"I'd like that." I slide my hand across to her shoulder and hold her against my side. "Let's take an extra plate from everyone and call it lunch."

"Ice cream lunch is something I can get down with." Joey rubs his hands together. "Welp, that's it for today, folks. Tune in tomorrow for the final challenge and to find out who will win the illustrious title of *Second Bite* champion."

ALICE

I tap my spoon against my lips as I savor the last bit of chai ice cream.

"I can see an idea brewing in your brain." Michael sets his plate on the coffee table in front of us. "What is it?"

"Well, Amber using our recipes has me thinking…" Michael tenses, and I shake my head, setting my plate down and turning on the couch to face him. "No, it's nothing bad. I was just thinking about the scholarship foundation idea. What if we did cooking classes as a way to raise money?"

His brows lift at my idea. "Cooking classes?"

I lift a shoulder. "It might be a dumb idea. We'd either have to do a ton of them or charge a ton of money, but if people like recreating our food…" I shrug again. "It's just an idea."

Michael is nodding. "It's a good idea. And people would definitely pay for it." He rubs his chin. "We could have it be ten grand a head. Have eight stations set up, with two people per station so couples or friends could sign up together."

My mouth drops open. "Ten thousand dollars a person?"

He just dips his chin, acknowledging my question while

blowing past it. Like ten freaking thousand dollars for a cooking class isn't the most absurd thing that's ever been suggested.

"We can pick different metro areas to offer them in, but if we do... eight... minus the cost of renting out the spaces and set up... We should be able to raise about a million dollars."

I blink at his math, then whisper, "A million dollars?"

Michael finally takes notice of my shock. "I know it sounds like a lot, but school is expensive. And if you figure around forty thousand as an average, that's only twenty-five kids getting a full ride. Or we can spread it out and do, I dunno, ten-grand scholarships to help with tuition instead of covering it. Then we can help a hundred kids."

He's tipping his head back and forth, doing the math, but my brain can't even keep up. Because all I can focus on is the love I have for this man.

"We could also—"

I don't hear whatever he's about to say because I launch myself across the couch at him.

I circle my arms around Michael's neck and hug him as tightly as I can. "I love you so much."

His chest rumbles against mine as he chuckles. "I love you too, Sweetness."

MICHAEL

I keep my steps light as I walk out of the bedroom and across the suite.

I feel bad sneaking out like this, but I couldn't think of a good excuse to leave earlier, and I have so much to do still.

Alice should sleep through the night though. She always does after a couple orgasms.

And it's not that I'm worried Alice would think I'm having an affair if she wakes up and finds me gone. Even with my ex-girlfriend in the building, Alice knows I have zero good feelings toward Amber. What had been indifference before has turned into true disdain after her behavior these last few days.

I just don't want Alice to wake up alone.

Ever.

So I'll need to work fast.

After quietly shutting the door behind me, I make my way downstairs to the hotel kitchen.

Not running into anyone, I use my key and unlock the door.

Then I turn on the lights and get to work.

ALICE

I burrow deeper into the scent of brown sugar and make a humming sound.

Heat wraps around me, an echoing sound of comfort coming from the body in front of mine.

"Morning." Michael's voice is gruff.

"Morning," I mumble against his chest before sniffing his shirt. "You smell like breakfast."

A hand slides down my back to palm my ass. "I bet you taste like breakfast."

I arch my back, pressing my ass into his hand.

Michael slaps it.

I let out a yelp, but my core pulses in response.

"Mr. Kesso," I chastise.

Michael groans and rolls over me.

My legs spread as I settle onto my back, making room for Michael and his length between my thighs.

"Call me that again." He rocks his hips, rubbing his cock against my core. My thin sleep shorts and his boxer briefs are the only barrier between us.

I grab his sides, holding him to me. "Are we going to practice for our cooking class, Mr. Kesso?"

A big hand reaches down and pinches my nipple through my tank top. "If the class gets to watch us do this, then we need to charge more."

A moan gets caught with a laugh in my throat. "Anything for the students, sir."

Michael groans and reaches lower.

I expect him to slide his hand inside the top band of my shorts, but he reaches lower.

My shorts are loose enough that he's able to pull the fabric between my legs over to one side, exposing the fact that I'm not wearing panties.

"Tsk, tsk, Ms. Hatter." The back of his fingers drag across my damp entrance. "Violating dress code on your first day of class."

Holy fucking snowflakes. Michael dirty talking is the hottest thing in the whole wide world.

My chest heaves. "Wh-What are you going to do to me, Mr. Kesso?"

"Punish you." He shifts, moving his hand away from my body. Then the hot tip of his dick slaps down against my slit. "With a pounding."

Michael shifts his hips, then slams into me.

And at the same time, my alarm starts to blare.

It's sensory overload.

My pussy is stretched around him.

My heart is galloping like a herd of reindeer in my chest.

And I can't even hold onto him because my muscles are too weak with pleasure.

"Best come for me quick, Ms. Hatter." Michael's breaths are ragged. "This is the third time your alarm has gone off. You're going to be late for class if you don't hurry up."

"Third time?" I pant.

Michael's hips are moving fast, pounding into me like he promised, and my pulse can't keep up.

Then I really register what he said, and I turn my head to look at the clock.

"Michael!"

He slams into me. "That's not what you call me, Ms. Hatter. Now rub your clit and tell me you're sorry."

Lust crashes over me, and I wedge a hand between us to do as I'm told.

"I'm sorry, Mr. Kesso." My bud is so sensitive that the moment my fingers connect, I feel myself climbing toward the crescendo. "I'm so sorry I misbehaved. Please don't make me late."

"That's a good girl." Michael's body tenses. He's just as close as I am. "Now make yourself come on my cock, Ms. Hatter, and I'll give you that A you want."

That shouldn't be hot.

Just like calling him Santa shouldn't have been hot.

But it is.

And I can't hold back anymore.

MICHAEL

I collapse on top of my girl.
My woman.

And even though I'm sure I'm crushing her, she makes a contented sound.

Then the beeping of the alarm breaks through the blood rushing through my ears.

Right. The show.

Alice must recognize the sound at the same time I do because she starts to push at my shoulders. "Michael, we need to shower."

Still buried inside her, I give my hips a shallow thrust. "I'd need a few minutes, but we could definitely do this again in the shower."

She moans, "Michael."

I sigh and reluctantly pull out of her sweet heat and flop onto my back. "Fine, you can go first."

She pats my arm as she shimmies out of bed. "You're the best."

She tries to keep her thighs pressed together but mumbles something about a mess as she shuffles into the bathroom.

As I work to catch my breath, I stare up at the ceiling.
A lot of things are going to change today.
My whole life is going to change today.
And I've never felt more sure of myself.
I fill my lungs, Alice's scent still clinging in the air.
And I smile.

ALICE

*T*he final challenge starts.

Each baker immediately goes to work on their celebration of New Year's desserts.

Michael and I walk hand in hand to each workstation.

We listen to their ideas. Each baker doing something different.

One hour ticks away.

Then the second.

And I soak it all in.

This will be my last day of judging.

I don't know if they'd even want me to continue on, but I already told the producers I wouldn't. I won't take Pamela's job. I couldn't do that to her or her fans.

Maybe when she decides to leave. *Maybe.* But I think I'll do better behind the scenes.

Joey calls out that there are thirty minutes left.

Michael and I sit in our chairs at the front of the room, and I do my best to remember the stupid microphone.

I do my best to keep my hands off him.

I do my best to ignore the ache between my legs.
Ten minutes left.
Five.
Two.
And it's done.

MICHAEL

We move away from Drake's station and over to Colby's.

"Remind us what you made." Alice takes the lead.

The comedian nods to the spherical cake before him. "This is a lemon and lime marble cake that I've covered in orange buttercream and glitter sugar candies to replicate the ball drop in Times Square."

It's gaudy, and I'm not convinced the candies are edible, but it certainly fits the theme. He even has a stick jutting out of the top, replicating the pole the ball slides down.

"It's fantastic." Alice clasps her hands in front of her, getting closer to the cake.

"Thank you." Colby beams. "But before you cut it..." He reaches under the counter and comes out with a lighter.

He ignites the flame, and that's when I realize what the stick in the middle of the cake is.

It's a fucking sparkler.

"I don't think—" Before I can finish, he's touched the flame to the sparkler.

Alice lets out a laugh of enjoyment when the sparks start flying. But then one of the sparks shoots straight down to the questionable candies covering the cake.

And the whole thing lights up into a miniature fireball.

I grip Alice's elbow and yank her away from the danger, but a candy flies off and lands on the loose sleeve of her bright white top.

The ember blooms as the fabric catches fire.

My heart seizes inside my ribs even as I move to react.

Lunging into her, I engulf her forearm with my hands, hugging it to my body, smothering the fire.

The sparkler is still going, sizzling down to the final inch, but the cake isn't in danger of catching fire again since the entire thing is scorched black.

Colby is standing several feet back from his bench, hands up in front of him in a protective manner.

I look beyond Colby to see Zelle with her hands against her cheeks and Amber fighting off a laugh.

Drake steps up beside us.

"You guys okay?" the movie star asks. "I've been burned a few times on set, so I know some tricks if either of you are hurt."

I loosen my grip on Alice's arm, slowly pulling away to reveal the hole burned into her sleeve.

"Are you hurt?" I struggle to get the words out, fear at seeing my woman lit up in flames still choking me.

"No." Alice reaches across to pluck at her sleeve. "Are you? Did my shirt burn you?"

I want to believe her, but...

I grip her sleeve on either side of the small burn hole and tear the fabric.

It gives way easily, the thin material splitting from her wrist to her shoulder.

"Michael!"

"I need to see." I say the only thing I can.

But when I run my eyes and hands over her arm, I don't find a single mark.

"Michael," she says again.

I drag my hands over her forearm again.

"Mr. Kesso," she sternly hisses.

And my eyes snap up to hers.

Her mouth pulls into a sneaky smile. "Show me your palms."

Calmer, I release her arm and hold my hands out, palms up.

She drags her fingertips over the sensitive skin but doesn't find any burn marks on me either.

The flaming candy must've fallen away as I pulled her against me.

"I'm sorry." Colby finally speaks up. "That wasn't supposed to happen."

Drake snorts a *no shit* before he turns and walks back to his station.

The sparkler finally putters out, and we all stare at the cake.

"We could, um, taste the inside," Alice says beside me.

A tendril of smoke comes up from the center of the cake.

"Or maybe not," she adds.

Colby grimaces. "So... what are the odds I could still win?"

Too pissed about him endangering Alice to joke, I turn away from Colby without another word and guide Alice to Zelle's station.

The girls spend a moment checking in on each other, and I let my heartbeat return to normal.

When they're certain they're both okay, I cut into the stunning fruit tart Zelle has made.

The shortcrust is perfect, the thin layer of peaches on top of the vanilla custard is delicious, and the glazed raspberries and pomegranate seeds are laid into the shape of an exploding firework across the surface.

It's perfectly crafted.

Everything Zelle has made has been delicious. And as long as Amber doesn't create something absolutely outstanding, I can select Zelle as the winner with a clear conscience.

ALICE

The salted caramel cheesecake that Amber made looks appealing, even if it does look like she's flooded the entire top with caramel.

She's used careful piping to write Happy New Year across the surface, but that's it.

It's simple. A little basic. But could still be delicious.

Michael slices into the dessert, and as he's pulling the slice away—the caramel dripping off the edges—I see him smirk.

It's just for a split second. The briefest of moments. But I saw it.

Michael is happy.

And then I see why.

The cheesecake is curdled.

Lumps mar what should be a silky smooth texture.

I take a bite, and it doesn't even matter that her salted caramel is way too salty. She won't win.

I don't like wishing ill will on people.

I want to be someone who supports everyone.

But there's an exception to every rule. And today, Amber is that exception.

Michael sets his fork down. "The caramel is too salty. The cheesecake mixture has curdled. And you needed to have blind baked that crust because it's soggy."

His words are harsh. Unforgiving. But that's how he always is to people who mess up, so it's not like he's being mean just because it's Amber. And it's not even really being mean if it's all true.

I set my fork down and smile at the soap opera star. "We all make mistakes sometimes."

Mine was the Jell-O scarf.

Hers was this cheesecake.

And Michael's was dating her.

MICHAEL

$\mathcal{I}$ shake Zelle's hand, congratulating her on her win.

And I let Alice see my raised brow when she moves in to give Zelle a big hug.

The cameras crowd in around us, and when Alice steps back, Colby and Drake move in to give Zelle hugs too.

I don't bother looking for Amber. It's no surprise that she's a sore loser. And now that the special is done, I don't have to pay her a single bit of attention for the rest of my life.

Alice stands beside me as Zelle brushes a tear off her cheek. "Sorry." She chuckles. "It feels so silly to cry, but this is the first non-singing competition I've ever won."

Joey grins. "Well, there's no more hiding the fact that you're an amazing baker. And if you ever get sick of singing, you could open a bakery."

Zelle shakes her head. "I know how early bakers have to get up. I'm not cut out for that."

Alice leans her head against my shoulder, and I entwine my fingers with hers.

She looks up at me, a gentle smile on her face. "I can't believe I got to be a judge on *Second Bite*."

"You're a natural at it," I tell her honestly.

Alice sighs. "Hopefully it came off that way because I'm pretty sure I was hyperventilating half the time."

I shake my head, even as my own nerves start to grow. "You were perfect." Then, seeing that Joey is done talking, I heave out a breath. "But we're not quite done yet."

Alice furrows her brows. "What do you mean?"

Joey moves to stand before me. "Ready for the next part?"

I nod, and, with my free hand, I pull my phone out of my pocket.

"What's going on?" Alice looks back and forth between me and Joey, who has turned on one of the large TV monitors on the wall.

I squeeze Alice's fingers. "Just taking care of some business." Then I hit the selection to make a video call on my phone.

As it rings, the TV monitor lights up with my image on one side and a blank image on the other.

Then my private investigator answers, and his face populates the other half.

"Afternoon, Mr. Kesso." His bushy mustache moves with each syllable.

"Hello, Mr. Forde. Are you in position?" I ask.

Nearly everyone on set is gaping at me, Alice included.

I didn't leave her out of my plans for any other reason than I didn't want to cause her any extra stress.

Once I was able to confirm that Joey had nothing to do with any of the schemes against me, I pulled him into my plans, and he happily agreed to help.

"I'm in sight and ready," my PI replies.

My smile is wicked. "Move ahead." Then I glance down at Alice, knowing the cameras and mics will pick up what I say to her. "Mr. Forde is the private investigator I hired. And he's been very productive."

"Oh," Alice says before her brows jump up. "Oh!"

I dip my chin back toward the screen.

Mr. Forde has turned the phone around so it shows where he's going.

And he's going to a middle-aged man sitting alone at a table inside a coffee shop.

The man has his laptop open in front of him and a plate covered in crumbs next to him.

Mr. Forde pulls out the only other chair at the small round table, and as he sits down, he presses the lid of the laptop shut.

The man jerks his hands out of the way. "What the—" Then he notices the phone. And my face staring back at him. "Michael?"

"You've been a hard man to reach," I tell my manager.

"What is this?" He tries to keep his tone even, but I can hear the panic.

"This is part of the show. Since you've decided to involve yourself so much over the past few days, I didn't think you'd mind the screen time."

"Screen time?"

I give a serious nod. "We're still live. And to all our viewers, I'd like to introduce you to my manager. The man who purposefully didn't tell me about the celebrity switch. The man who told casting to put Amber Addison on the show. The same man who talked to the producers two nights ago to tell them I wanted the middle challenge changed to ice cream." I hear a few gasps from the crew around me.

"That was for ratings. It's not personal." My manager tries to justify. "And it's not like it cost you anything to have a little bit of drama."

I grit my teeth. "Your actions caused my woman emotional stress. And that alone is enough for me to end your career."

"End my career?" He raises his voice, then looks around the coffee shop and lowers it. "After all these years, you're going to fire me over this?"

"I'm not going to fire you over Amber and ice cream." His shoulders relax. "But I am going to fire you over the photos."

The world watches as my manager's face pales.

He thought he got away with that.

He thought I only knew about the show shit.

Maybe even tried to distract me with all this Amber bullshit.

But he'd be wrong.

I look down at Alice, whose eyes are wide. "This is the man responsible for our photos being plastered all over the tabloids."

"Your manager? Why?" she asks quietly.

"That's a good question. And it's one I asked Mr. Forde." I look back at the screen. "Seems my lovely manager has had a bit of a spending problem. Too many lavish vacations and fender benders in expensive vehicles. And according to an email recovered from Mr. Forde—to the photographer—my manager had a suspicion I was considering firing him." I sigh. "Which I'll admit is true."

Alice lets out a little snort at my insincere tone.

"I didn't—"

I cut my soon-to-be ex-manager off. "You did. And you did it over email." I shake my head. "Mr. Forde could've dug the emails out, but he didn't even have to. The man you hired to take the photos handed them over, along with his portion of the money you made selling the images." I squeeze Alice's hand. "And we're using that money as the first donation to the *Second Bite* Scholarship Fund. And while Alice and I enjoy our New Year's, you better get back on that laptop and file for unemployment because you're fired."

A hand moves into the frame from behind the camera and drops a cloth bag onto the table.

The sound is loud through the microphone.

"What's this?" My ex-manager glares at the bag.

"Your severance," I tell him. "It's a bag of coal."

Then I hang up.

ALICE

I feel oddly turned on as Michael slides his phone back into his pocket.

I think we need to revisit the instructor role-playing again tonight.

"Joey, I'm ready for the next part," Michael calls out.

My attention turns to Joey as he opens a pair of doors I hadn't noticed before.

Through it, two people wheel in a table holding a three-tier square cake that looks to be entirely covered in gold leaf.

"What's the next part?" I whisper.

"The next part," Michael whispers back as he pulls on my hand to bring me closer to the cake, "is the rest of our lives."

Emotions tie a ribbon around my throat, making it hard to swallow.

And as we get closer, I notice the words etched into the gold.

The love of my life.

My forever.

Baby Cakes.

Little Alice.

Mrs. Claus.

Mistletoe Eyes.

My Sweetness.

Then I hear it.

The chimes.

My eyes slowly lift, and I watch Joey carefully set something on the top of the cake.

A shiny round gold centerpiece, with candles around the bottom and angels twirling above the flames.

It's the same.

It is the exact same centerpiece that my grandmother would put out for Christmas.

The same thing that I drew for Michael days ago when we were snowed in at that cabin.

It's exactly the same... except for the flash of color, the red and green sparkling in the candlelight on each turn.

Michael lets go of my hand and reaches up to stop the angels from spinning.

And from the top of an angel's head, he picks up a ring.

My hands press over my heart.

And my vision swirls as tears fill my eyes.

Michael gives me the softest smile as he lowers to one knee before me. "Alice." He holds up the ring. The massive princess-cut diamond is set in a band of alternating rubies and emeralds. "I know I've only just met you. And I know this is fast. But I don't need years to know that you're mine. I felt it the moment I laid eyes on you. I can feel the truth of it right here." He places a palm over his heart. "It's the same place I can feel your love for me. It's burrowed there. Made itself a home inside me. You give me warmth. Purpose. And I need the entire world to know it will only ever be you." He lifts his hand from his chest and holds it out to me. "So tell me, Baby Cakes, will you marry me?"

"Of course." I'm nodding and sniffing. "I will."

Michael holds my hand steady with one of his.

He slides the ring onto my finger. "Good. Because we're going to do it on New Year's Eve."

My eyes widen, and a laugh bubbles out of me as I throw my arms around my Chef.

EPILOGUE 1

ALICE

*M*y cousins both wipe tears from their eyes, and I use a tissue to dab at my own.

When I asked them, Suzy and Sam immediately agreed to walk me down the aisle, which we're about to do.

But it was their decision to wear matching black tuxes.

"You look like you belong in a fairytale." Sam sniffles.

I look down at my red satin dress.

The long sleeves are loose but collared at my wrists, and the neckline plunges almost indecently low. And at my side is a bow, where the sides of the dress tie together.

As my cousins each take a side and we start to walk forward, the skirt splits around my leg, exposing my thigh.

And when Michael comes into view and looks at me like that, I feel like the most beautiful woman in the world.

MICHAEL

When Alice stops before me in the room decorated with twinkling lights and filled with the handful of people who are truly important to us, all I can think about is how perfect it all is.

The place.

The time.

The woman.

"Can I go first?" Alice asks. And I dip my chin.

She presses her lips together, and I grip her hands in mine.

"I can't tell you how many times I fantasized about this day. How many times I closed my eyes at night and wished you were by my side. How many moments of my days I spent thinking of you." My chest tightens at her words. "I've loved you for so long, Chef Michael. But even with my birthday wishes, the most I ever wished for was your happiness." She smiles up at me, and my heart grows with each of her words. "All I've ever wanted was for you to be happy." I hold her hands tighter. "I can see it in your eyes, you know? When you look at me, like you are right now, I can see that—by some miracle of the universe—it's me who makes you happy." A single tear trails down Alice's cheek, and it mirrors my own. "You're my real-life fairytale, Mr. Kesso. And this is my real-life happily ever after."

ALICE

"Where are we going?" I can't stop my giggle as Michael hauls me away from our reception and into an elevator.

I may have had too much champagne tonight, especially after those Jell-O shots Suzy snuck into the venue. But is it really possible to have too much at your wedding? Especially when it's New Year's Eve?

Michael smirks down at me as he presses the button for the top floor.

It's the penthouse suite. The biggest, most over-the-top hotel room I've ever laid eyes on.

But I wouldn't care if we were going back to my basement bedroom. The only thing that matters is that it's my wedding night and I'm spending it with Michael.

The elevator doors slide shut, and Michael steps back so he can look at all of me.

"You're fucking beautiful, Mrs. Kesso."

Warmth fills my belly.

"You're not too bad yourself, Mr. Kesso."

It's an understatement. In head-to-toe black, Michael looks the perfect mix of handsome and dangerous.

The doors slide open.

"Come, Wife."

I take Michael's hand and resist making a comment about how I plan to.

We walk in silence to our door, and I wait for Michael to unlock it.

We stayed here last night, in the suite overlooking Minneapolis, so I know what to expect when the door opens.

Except it's not exactly the same.

The lights are all dimmed, and there are overflowing bouquets of flowers in the living room.

I slow, spotting a tray of chocolate-covered berries and a bottle of champagne on the coffee table.

Michael starts to pull me past it, then he pauses.

"Actually..." He reaches down and plucks the bottle out of the bucket of ice. "Now come on, we're almost out of time."

"Out of time?" I quicken my steps to keep up with him.

"You'll see." Michael doesn't turn toward the bedroom. He leads me to the doors to the rooftop terrace.

He drags the door open, and a gust of cold air rolls over us.

I'm about to tell him it's too cold to go outside when I see it.

The dome-shaped tent.

Only it's not a tent exactly, because, as I step out into the night, the city lights bounce off the mirrored walls of the dome.

"We can see out," Michael says as he unzips a hidden door panel. "But no one can see in."

Desire starts to swirl in my center.

I have an idea of what Michael would like to do out here, and I'm ready for it.

When I step inside the little dome, I'm surprised by the warmth—the dim glow of a heater in the corner.

And the rest of the space is filled with... a bed covered in thick blankets and fluffy pillows.

Michael follows me in and secures the door.

"Take your panties off, Mrs. Kesso."

I turn to face him, the bed behind me.

Slowly, I part the sides of my skirt, revealing more and more skin as I go.

Michael shrugs off his suit jacket as he watches.

I reach up under my dress and grip the sides of my panties.

Michael undoes the top two buttons of his shirt.

I tug the lacy material down my legs.

Michael rolls up his sleeves.

I step out of my panties.

Michael holds his hand out for them.

Heat blooms inside me as I place the body-warmed fabric into his hand.

He closes his fist around the material, then shoves them into his pocket. "Sit on the edge of the bed."

I sit.

He removes his belt.

I spread my knees, my skirt splitting to the hip, the material draping between my legs.

He undoes his pants, the zipper loud in the small space.

I reach for the tie at my side.

He pulls the front of his boxer briefs down.

I undo the bow, and the dress loosens, then parts. And my bare breasts spill free.

Michael groans and pulls his dick out.

I stare. My mouth watering.

"Eyes up here." His voice is gravel.

I lift my gaze to meet Michael's as he opens the champagne.

It's dark, but not so dark I can't see his expression.

The hunger in his eyes.

And it's making me tremble.

"Husband, I need you to touch me."

Michael steps between my spread legs, his cock straining toward me.

Strong fingers grip my chin, tipping my head back just a bit more.

"Open your mouth, Wife."

I part my lips. But instead of feeding me his length, Michael brings the champagne bottle up to his mouth.

He swallows, then pours more into his mouth. And dampness pools between my legs.

I get it now.

I open my mouth wider.

He bends over me, and with his eyes on mine, he parts his lips, and the champagne falls from his mouth into mine.

And the sky erupts above us.

Fireworks fill the night.

The taste. The explosions. All of it lights my body on fire.

Michael applies pressure on my chin. "Swallow."

I close my mouth and swallow.

Michael lowers to his knees before me.

The low bed is the perfect height. And his body lines up with mine.

Michael holds the bottle up to my mouth as he presses the tip of his dick against my wet entrance.

I tip my head back again, and this time he pours the liquid directly into my mouth.

I keep it there.

The bubbles dancing on my tongue.

Michael sets the bottle down, then grabs my hip with one hand and the back of my head with the other.

Michael tilts his mouth below mine.

I press my lips to his parted ones, and as I push the champagne out of my mouth and into his, he shoves his hips forward.

He fills me as he takes from me.

He fucks me as he makes love to me.

And under the exploding sky, we melt into each other.

Becoming one.

EPILOGUE TWO

MICHAEL

"*H*urry!" Alice calls from the study.

"I'm right here, Baby." I step through the doorway, two glasses of wine in hand.

Alice looks up from her spot on the couch, snuggled under her favorite blanket with a laptop balanced on her lap. "Oh, good idea." She takes the glass I hold out for her.

Careful not to spill, I slide into the spot next to Alice and prop my feet on the coffee table.

It's been three months since Alice became my wife, and every day is better than the last.

Even with filming only now starting up again for *Second Bite*, we've been busy since the New Year started—traveling, getting the foundation ready.

So, as a way to celebrate the launch of the Chef Mike and Alice Cooking Classes, we decided to rent a place in the mountains.

Alice suggested going back to the cabin in Bear Cove, but we both agreed we could find something with the same feel that doesn't also have the creeper memories.

Though, to be fair, since Mr. Forde has recovered the backlist of photos, we have looked through them. Many times. Without clothes on. So it's not all bad.

I drape my arm over the back of the couch behind Alice.

This is just a rental house, but I think I'll put an offer on it. Our lives are only going to get busier after tonight, and having a little forest retreat might be just the thing.

"One minute." Alice chews her lip.

I squeeze her shoulder. "Did they confirm that our end of the site would update in real time?"

We did what we discussed, selecting eight cities across the country to host classes, and now it's just a matter of filling the spots.

Alice nods but still hits the refresh button on the website. "Yeah. The sale will open on the hour, first come, first served." She blows out a breath. "What if no one signs up? It's so expensive."

"People will sign up, Baby Cakes. We might not sell out in the first five minutes like a Zelle concert, but we'll fill every seat, I promise."

"I really hope so," Alice says.

A second later, the clock in the corner of her screen clicks over.

"It's live," she whispers.

We stare at the screen, the crackling fireplace across the room the only thing breaking the silence.

I open my mouth to remind her I'm proud of her. To tell her that no matter how long it takes, I love her so much.

But before I can say anything, the column for Minneapolis lights up.

A moment later, the first name appears, claiming two tickets. *Mr. and Mrs. Eklund.*

Alice squeaks. "We sold a pair!"

Another set populates.

Mr. and Mrs. Vass.

Alice gasps.

Then another couple.

Mr. and Mrs. Gonzalez.

Alice lifts a hand to her mouth.

Another two tickets are sold. A singular name on both.

Nero.

I turn to Alice, lifting my glass to tap against hers. "Looks like our first class will be in Minnesota."

AUTHOR'S NOTE

You read that right.

The Alliance men are taking their women to a cooking class.
Taught by Alice and Chef Michael.

Stay tuned…

XOXO

Follow me on Amazon for updates about new releases!

ACKNOWLEDGMENTS

Happy holidays to all my readers. Chances are you're reading this sometime between November and December, and you've probably spent a lot of time around family and/or coworkers and friends... and you probably needed a break from it all. (Like for real. The holidays can be a lot for a lot of reasons.) So thank you for taking some of your valuable time to join me in a Tilly World adventure. If you've read *Smoky Darling, Latte Darling, Dom...* hopefully it was a nice little treat to get to see some "behind the curtains" of the *Second Bite* TV show.

As always, I need to thank my mother, Karen. Thank you for all your hard work beta and alpha reading. And also for instilling me with a love of the holidays. Christmas always meant family, food, and Santa. And there was only that one time when *he* left a bag of rocks in my Santa Sack because, apparently, I'd been extra bratty that year. (I know, readers, it's hard to imagine!) (Also, a Santa Sack is just a giant stocking with a drawstring. Don't make it fucking weird.)

Thank you, Jeanine, for being my rescue editor and always fitting me into your schedule. I appreciate you so much! And thank you Beth for always making me look so smart.

Thank you to my cover designers for this series, Lori and James. And thank you to Wander and his team for taking this amazing photo for me. It's perfection.

Thank you, Kerissa, for being my beta reader, alpha reader, PA and friend. And for encouraging me to add more Christmas puns. You weren't wrong, and I love you.

And, of course, thank you to my ARC team. Your support seriously makes my life so much better.

Thank you to my husband, who has probably never read an acknowledgment page in his life, but nonetheless, I appreciate your encouragement and the fact that you listen to me explain the recipes in this book, in extreme detail, even though I'm sure you'd rather have done anything else.

And lastly, thank you to my grandmother, the origin of the Tilly name, for all your Norwegian baking. Christmas hasn't been the same without you and without your homemade krumkake. These cloudberries are for you.

ABOUT THE AUTHOR - S.J. TILLY

S.J. Tilly was born and raised in Minnesota, which is why so many of her books are based there. But she now resides in the beautiful mountains of Colorado with her husband and misfit herd of rescue boxers.

She spends an unhealthy amount of time with her face buried in books, either reading or writing. And if she's not nose-deep in text or harassing her dogs (and it's not the dead of winter), you can probably find her playing with her plants, pretending she knows how to garden. Even if her yard is a hot-flowery mess, at least the bees are happy! To stay up to date on all things Tilly, make sure to follow her on her socials, join her newsletter, and interact whenever you feel like it! Links to everything on her website: www.sjtilly.com

ALSO BY

The Alliance Series

(Dark Mafia Romance)

NERO

KING

DOM

HANS

The Sin Series

(Romantic Suspense)

MR. SIN

SIN TOO

MISS SIN

The Darling Series

(Small Town Age Gap)

SMOKY DARLING

LATTE DARLING

The Sleet Series

(Hockey Rom Com)

SLEET KITTEN

SLEET SUGAR

SLEET BANSHEE

SLEET PRINCESS

The Bite Series

(Holiday Novellas - Baking Competition)

SECOND BITE

SNOWED IN BITE

NEW YEAR'S BITE

The Mountain Men Series (coming 2025)